MALE of the SPECIES

Alex Mindt

Delphinium Books

Harrison, New York • Encino, California

FIRST EDITION

Library of Congress Cataloguing-in-Publication Data is available upon request.

Library of Congress Control Number: 2007921883

ISBN: 1-883285-28-3

For Monica, Laurel Grace,
and Truman

My gratitude goes out to the editors of the following publications where these stories originally appeared:

Sabor a Mi—Willow Springs
Reception—Confrontation
An Artist at Work—Carve Magazine
Stories of the Hunt—Literary Review
Male of the Species—The Missouri Review
The Gypsy—Indy Men's Magazine
King of America—Night Train
Free Spirits—The Sun
Immigration—Fiction
Karrooo—The Missouri Review

"Sabor a Mi" also appeared in the 2006 Puschart Prize Anthology.

Thanks to all the teachers who taught me the things I needed to learn (and the things I didn't) at Beverly Elementary, Meadowdale Middle School, Meadowdale High School, Carnegie Mellon

University, the University of Iowa and Columbia University. A special thanks to Jaime Manrique, Austin Flint, Jessica Hagedorn, Barbara MacKenzie-Wood, Bob Burton, Charles Lewarne, Helen MacGilvra, Ginny Enstad, Joyce Hudemann, Lucy Anderson, Mr. Bray, Mrs. Hoff, Don Haase, Carol Doerschlag, Paul Diehl, Oliver Steele, John Harper, and Richard Locke. To all of my workshop mates at Columbia who courageously slogged through the muck of my early drafts, to my brothers Bruce and Brian, and to my dad and grandpa for showing me what a man is and what a father does, to Randall Harvey, my first workshop partner, for our time in the trenches, to Bob and Van, for direction and indirection, to Cyndi, Maggie, Eric, and David for your continued support, to David Plante for awareness and ostrananie, and to Bill Crossett, my lifelong mentor, who showed me early on what an artist is, to all of you I am grateful. To my agent Kimberley Cameron, who never stopped believing, to Adam Marsh for his keen eyes and his hard work, to Barbara Ascher, my editor who heard my voice and gave it clarity, I appreciate you all so much. To my mother, who filled our home with books and music, what can I say? ¡A Monica, por darme esta vida, muchas gracias!

Contents

"Men must endure their going hence, even as they're coming hither."

—Shakespeare

"What Americans fear is the inability to have a world like their father's . . ."

—Lynne Tillman

"I looked out my window to see where my father might be hiding."

—Ben Marcus

"Remember, as far as anyone knows, we're a nice normal family."

—Homer Simpson

MALE of the SPECIES

Sabor a Mí

The song says, "So much time we have enjoyed this love." But songs aren't life. What do you do when your grown daughter, a mother of two, comes to you and says she wants to be now with women? I am old, too old for this. So I tell her to leave and I will pray. My whole life I pray and look around, what good has it done? What do I have? My son, my first son, Juan Jr., in Los Angeles, his body found in a car under the freeway. My second son, Javier, sent back from Vietnam in a bag, for nothing.

In Mexico you don't lose your family, even after they die. Here everyone is alone. Loneliness made this country. When you are lonely, you either find some way to kill yourself or you work hard and make money. People here, they either die or they become rich.

When I was fourteen I waded across the Rio Grande at Ojinaga and saw this country from the back of a pickup truck, picking sugar beets in Minnesota, apples in Wenatchee. In Ventura there were strawberries. In Calabasas, tomatoes. Figs in Palm Springs. Cotton in Arizona and Texas. Now I live in New Mexico. Many years have passed. I saved and saved until I had my own small restaurant and raised my family. I insisted they speak perfect English. Now not one of them speaks Spanish. When I talk to them I have to think about every word.

I do not have a home. I have this facility, in Santa Fe, the second-oldest city in America. My youngest boy, Mario, he pays for this place. He owns a body repair shop in Albuquerque. Every month I get a check. But does he come out? Does he take his *gringa* wife and their kids to see their papi? Last year, I went down to his big house for Lori's *quinceañera*. But where was the *pan dulce*? The dancing? After a few minutes, the kids, they get in their cars and drive off. My son, he just shrugs.

Last week I received a letter in the mail. It was from my daughter. There was a picture of her and a dog and another woman. The dog had long ears. The woman had short hair. Inside was an invitation to a wedding. I had to read it several times.

My daughter, Raquel, wants now to marry this woman. Her first husband was named Charlie. Her second will be named Diane. Raquel was so smart. She learned English so fast. And then in school she learned French and could speak that too. But not Spanish. She went to Paris and became a cook like her father. Only what she makes, with those thick creams, I don't eat so much.

Rosalinda, what do you say to me now? I wait for your voice when the noise fades and the crickets sing. But you are silent. Why won't you speak to me? I live in a facility now, Rosi. For my sadness, the nurses, they give me pills. I still think of that day, climbing down the fig tree. You were at the meal truck, holding a stainless steel tray, the sun shining twice on your lovely skin. I remember your long black hair pulled back tight, and the mark of dirt on your forehead, and how all I could do was smile and look away.

Rosi, I know what you would say. But Raquel wants to love this woman, and I say no. She has a son and a daughter, you remember Stephen and Elizabeth? But who listens to me? She did not ask my permission. Am I not her father? I do not know my own children. They move around me like ghosts.

The food here is hatred on my tongue. Eggs and toast too hard to chew, not even the beans have flavor. But I am leaving now. I have eaten breakfast. I have put on my good suit, and now Raquel will hear what I have to say. The gate is open in the back behind the piñon tree, and outside the cars are rushing. A river of steel and rubber roars past. It is late morning, but the sun is rising fast in the sky. I will walk until darkness, and then I will keep walking if I have to. Outside Santa Fe the air is dry and sweet from the lavender and poppies. The sign says *Taos 78 Miles*. I will walk 78 miles if I have to.

I do not hold out my hand. Cars will stop. An old man, walking a highway, a slumped, old man, surely someone will stop and ask where I'm going. Gringos are not all bad. They clean up after themselves and act nice, even if they don't mean it.

I need you now, Rosalinda, for I have walked a long time and the sun is pushing down on me. The road is uphill. In a car you don't notice so much. But when the foot comes down, the ground is so much closer than when the foot came up. I have walked almost to the Indian reservation outside of town. Cars and trucks do not see me.

The dirt on the roadside is hard and dry, and the ravine beside me is full of rocks and no water. In this country, rivers and streams, they dry up. The sky takes our lives away. We become clouds. When it rains I see all the people who've gone before me. Mami, Papi, my baby boys. I see *Tío* Julio on a mattress under an apple tree, playing a guitar with only three strings. There are black birds and rotting apples.

But I don't see you, Rosi, and every time it rains I ask, what is wrong? What did I do? I would like it to rain now. It is so hot. Sweat is now bubbling up under this wool suit I still have, this suit you bought for me, for Raquel's quinceañera so many years ago. Do you remember Tío Julio and his band playing "Sabor a Mí" in the darkness, and how we danced? Do you remember the lovely noise of that night and the sangria, how the neighbors came over and then more and more until our yard was full of dancing?

I need a car to pull off now. My knees are burning with every step. I will stop and wait here until someone pulls over. This is a country made of rushing. Here, no one is anywhere, they are in between places. Only the dead are content.

Voices are singing from the shrubs and red stones. *"Tanto tiempo disfrutamos de este amor."* Even the cars sing as they rush by. *"Nuestras almas se acercaron tanto asi."* And I have to sit down. There is a pale rock, a large stone. Its shadow goes down the hill by the dried-up river.

Behind me the wind rises up, and a car pulls off the road. It is green, covered in dust, like a fig tree. A gringo gets out and looks at me over the roof, his light hair blowing sideways in the wind. "Hey," he says. And then he says something else. But a truck passes, and I can't hear him. And then he comes around the car and opens the door. He is kind of fat in the chest, with thin, pale legs, and he wears sandals, brown shorts, and a flowered shirt that hangs open over a white T-shirt. "I came by a minute ago and saw you walking," he says. "Thought I'd double back and see if you needed a lift. You okay?"

He wipes off the seat for me, and he tells me to push some buttons under my legs to be more comfortable. But I am fine.

"My name's Peter." He holds out his hand to me.

"I am Juan."

"Juan. That's John, right? In English, I mean."

"Yes." Inside the car cold air is blowing at me.

"This a little cold for you?" he says. "Here, let me crank this down a bit." He turns a dial. "As you can see, I like my air conditioned." He turns the steering wheel and goes onto the highway. "You want something to drink? Water, beer? You look a little thirsty."

"No, thank you."

Sunlight bounces off the car's green hood, and voices come out of a small speaker on the dashboard. *"What's your 10-20, Wayward Juice? Wayward Juice, you read me?"*

The gringo, Peter, he frowns at the speaker. "This guy's been calling for Wayward Juice all morning. Don't know why I bought this stupid CB, thought it would keep me company, I guess."

The tops of the mountains are white in the distance ahead of us.

"So, where you heading, Juan?"

"Taos."

"No kidding? Well, serendipity-do, so am I! I hope you're not in a hurry, cuz I was planning on taking the scenic route."

"I have to be there by seven."

"Oh, well, we've got some time then." He speaks very fast, this gringo. "So, why are you walking up to Taos on a hot day like this?"

"For a funeral." I do not know why I say it. God forgive me.

But how do you tell someone that your daughter is marrying a woman?

"I'm sorry to hear that," he says. "I hate it when people die. Was this person close to you?"

I turn my head and look out the window.

"Well, I'm sorry about that. I'm real sorry." He holds up his can of beer. "How 'bout a toast? To those who've come before, who've paved the way, and showed us how to live." He drinks his beer and places it between his legs.

"Horny Buzzard, we got a Kojak with a Kodak in a plain white wrapper."

Peter chuckles and shakes his head. "You hear that?" he says. "Man, they say the funniest things. 'Kojak with a Kodak.' I don't get half of it."

He turns onto the road that goes through the mountains, the high road, they call it. "I have to go the scenic route," he says. "I just can't stand those freeways. Freeways are just beginnings and endings. You know what I'm saying? You're either leaving a place or arriving at another place. And really there's nothing in between. I've been reading some books lately, you know, things I never read in college. Never had any use for them until now, I guess. But let me ask you, Juan, do you think it's a coincidence that the transcontinental freeways were being constructed at the precise time that existentialism had its greatest hold on the American psyche?"

I look out the window. Piñon trees are green spots on the hills around us.

"No comment, huh? I mean, don't get me wrong. America is great, right? The greatest country in the world. But there's something missing, isn't there? That's what I've found, and you know where I found it?"

"The freeways."

"Yes!" he says. "The freeways. They're like an empty stomach, you know, and it just wants and wants and wants." He reaches under the seat and pulls out another can of beer. "You sure you don't want anything to drink? They're getting kinda warm."

"No, thank you."

"You know what, Juan? This is my first time in the Southwest, and it's beautiful, it's flippin' unbelievable, the mountains, the sky. I know what you're thinking. I'm one of those crazy gringos, right? A car full of crap, driving all over hell? Yeah, well." He smiles and shakes his head. "I got this friend, Gary. Now Gary's a computer guy, you know, one of those Coke-bottle glasses type, all hunched over half the time, jerking off three times a day to some porno Web site, *motherjugs.com*, that sort of thing. He's got a *shooo-wing* for old ladies with big *cowangas*, if you get my drift. But don't get me wrong, Gary's brilliant, just like, wow, his brain, and he talks about systems, how things work, interconnected grids and all that, you know, overload and whatnot, and the truth of the matter, Juan, is, well, my wife left me a couple weeks ago. Took the kids with her. So I just got in the car and put my foot on the pedal. My hard drive just overloaded, as Gary would say. My fire-wall, or whatever, was just burning up. You're the first person I've had the chance to really talk to. Lucky you, huh? This CB, nobody wants to talk about real stuff. Just like police warnings or scary sex talk. I mean, some real unpleasant doo-doo." He smiles and blows out air. "That's what Tyler calls it. My son. He's twelve and he still calls it doo-doo."

He is quiet for a while, humming to himself, tapping the steering wheel with his fingers. "Hey," he says, "you know about this church up a ways? What's it called?" He reaches down for some papers. The car begins to swerve. "It's down here somewhere." All over the road, we are swerving. He finds the paper and grabs the steering wheel. "Whoa!" he says. "Ride 'em, cowboy!" He straightens the car out. "Anyway, like two hundred years ago," he says, "or something like that, this friar was digging and he found a crucifix, this miraculous crucifix in the dirt, and then they built a church around this pit, and over the years several miracles have been documented. I don't normally believe in that stuff. But then again, I don't normally just hop in my car and haul ass around the country."

He keeps talking. He talks and talks, but he is fine. Strangers will say things to you your family would never say. He tells me that he is afraid of heights and the ocean. And then he says, "Have you ever felt so sad that you can't feel anything? Have you ever just done something, just anything, I mean stupid things too, well, mainly stupid things really, to just maybe show yourself that you're still alive?"

I don't answer. We drive past a gringo market selling *Native Arts and Crafts,* and a restaurant with a sign that says *Savor the Flavor.* I think of Raquel, and how after coming back from France she told me there's more to flavor than chile and salt. "Why not use all the spices available to us?" she said. Then she said I was limited, I never opened my mind. I remember all the shouting and yelling, and never knowing why she was so angry at me. "With my limited money," I told her, "I gave you everything you wanted." And now she cooks snails.

Peter talks on and on until we drive through the Nambé Indian Reservation. He goes off the road and stops at a small adobe church, brown and leaning this way and that. "Hey," he says. "You want to take a look?"

"No, thank you," I say.

"Okay. I'll only be a minute." He takes a silver camera from the backseat and starts clicking photos.

Raquel is right now preparing for her wedding. The first one, so many years ago, in the church of St. Francis de Assisi, she took my arm, and my whole body shook, she was so beautiful. Her wavy black hair was all up on her head, and her white dress dragged on the ground behind her, like a queen. As I look down now, I cannot believe it, but this is the same suit I wore to her first wedding. And there is the button you sewed on, Rosi, that looks almost like the other buttons. Hush, you said, nobody will notice one silly button.

Peter gets back into the car and says, "That sucked. No one's around, and I couldn't get in." Peter puts the car back onto the highway and says, "Atheists for Jesus!" and punches the roof with his fist.

A voice comes from the speaker. *"10–11, Blutarski! 10–11!"*

Peter looks down at the radio and then at me. "I wonder what 10-11 means," he says.

"I said, that's a 10–42 Apache Bob. We got a meat wagon on yardstick 39."

He leans forward and turns off the radio. "A meat wagon. You think that's like a meal truck, Juan? Cuz I'm getting kind of hungry. Maybe they're selling sandwiches or tacos." Peter keeps talking about what he likes to eat, spaghetti, pot roast, what his mother used to make him when he and his brothers and sisters would come in from playing in the park. He talks, this gringo, like no gringo I've met, until we make it to the dusty junkyards of Chimayo, where everything has been left for dead. He stops in the parking lot of the shrine at El Santuario de Chimayo.

"This is it," he says. "The church I was telling you about, with the pit and the miracles. This is a sacred place." He opens the door. "Come on, I'll buy you something to eat."

There is a burrito stand, a restaurant, and a gift shop that sells T-shirts and refrigerator magnets in the shape of the shrine. Tourists bump into each other, looking at postcards and coasters. Peter talks to people he doesn't know, people behind the counter as he pays for postcards and T-shirts. Against the wall there is a large stuffed dog wearing jeans and a cowboy hat sitting in a chair with a pistol in his hand. *Cowboy Dog,* the sign says.

In the sacristy of the church there is a small round pit with a mound of dirt to the side. Crutches of wood and aluminum hang on the wall along with rosary beads, pictures of the sick and lame with letters and handmade shrines and crucifixes.

Peter points down to the mound of dirt. "This soil is supposed to be magical. It has healing powers, they say." He looks at me and smiles. "I don't believe any of that crap," he whispers. "But I'm definitely feeling something in here."

I get down on my knees at the pit and close my eyes. I am not praying exactly. But I want to listen, Rosi, for your voice. I spend my days talking to you, my love, but I can never hear you. Maybe your voice will come to me here. I think of those other women. Is that why you are silent? I know I was wrong, but that was so long ago, and I never speak to them, or think of them. They meant nothing, Rosi. I wasn't easy to be with, I know. But what about you? After the children left, and the house was empty, you wouldn't speak to me, and I know why. That was how you did it, Rosi. That was how you punished me. But please, *mi amor*, please know that I loved you as best I could.

When I open my eyes, Peter is sitting beside me with his eyes closed. He is a funny gringo. The wind has taken hold of him.

He opens his eyes and whispers, "You feeling anything, Juan?"

"Yes."

"Really? What do you think it is?"

"Pain," I say. "My knees. Will you help me up?"

Before we leave, Peter takes a picture of me at the pit, and then he asks a gringa to take a picture of us in front of the wall of crutches and shrines. He puts his arm around me and smiles.

Back in the car Peter eats a burrito while he drives. He says that there is definitely something back there. He holds up his can of beer. "A toast," he says. "To history, to all those who have come before us, to all those searching like we are, Juan."

"Salud," I say.

He drinks from the can. A piece of yellow cheese hangs off his chin.

"If you don't mind my asking," he says, "whose funeral are you going to?"

I do not know what to say. Whose funeral? I tell him, I don't know why, that I am going to my daughter's funeral. God forgive me.

"I'm sorry to hear that," he says. "I'm sorry. You must be devastated."

"At one time, we were very close."

"What was her name?"

"Raquel," I say.

"She must have been very special."

"She was my baby. And I loved her more than the others. But everything she ever did, it seemed like she wanted to disappoint me." I don't know why I say these things.

He nods and then is silent for a while.

"There is cheese on your chin," I say.

We drive through the villages of Truchas and Las Trampas. There are fields of blue flowers. Out my window a dirt road swerves between piñon trees, up a distant hill, and ends at a large white cross that stands against the pale blue sky.

"You ever been to the Church of St. Francis Assisi, Juan?"

"Yes. Many years ago."

"So, is it as spectacular as the photos and paintings?"

"I don't know."

"I've seen the pictures, you know, Ansel Adams, Georgia O'Keeffe. It's something I've always wanted to see. Some atheist, huh?"

I don't tell him that yes, I have made this drive before, that years ago we all drove up to the Church of St. Francis de Assisi, that my wife and sons were in the car with me, and that we were going to my daughter's first wedding.

When he stops in the square in Ranchos de Taos, he sits silently staring out the window at the giant church, at its round buttresses and thick vigas. There are many cars parked here and many people in work clothes standing outside the church.

"Wow," Peter says. "This is incredible." He gets out of the car and stands by the white cross in front of the church and stares up at the two bell towers.

I remember the irises and columbine, the petunias and roses. It was a spring night, like this. Remember, Rosi? Remember Raquel with flowers in her hair and the church full of family and friends from Texas, California, Arizona? Remember Tío Jorgé, the

Garcias, the Tofoyas, little Juan Armijo, Dale Seaver, Renata, Pilar, and their families, José and Felicia, and Charlie's gringo friends and family? Remember the lights in the square and the mariachi band with the violins, trumpets, bassos, and guitars? And the singing! Oh, those voices! How we danced that night under the candles and the string of lights!

Peter comes back to the car and says, "I forgot my camera." He reaches into the backseat. "They're mudding the damn thing. The people, they're all slapping mud on it."

He leaves the car and begins taking pictures of the golden church. I get out and walk up to the flower beds by the white cross and look up at the bell towers. All around, there are people, young and old, gringo and Latino, adding to the church's giant walls. It is like a woman. There are no sharp angles, only curves, and over the years she gets bigger but only grows more beautiful.

"Hey, Juan," Peter says, "turn around. Let's get you in the picture." He snaps his camera and says, "That will be really nice, by the cross, with the bell tower in the background." He points at the people with mud on their hands. "They say they're renewing the church. Everyone gets together and does this renewal thing. They've learned how from the people who came before and will pass it on to those who will come later. Tradition," he says, holding up his can of beer. "Ritual!"

I nod at Peter and then go into the church, where it is quiet and cool. There are paintings on the walls, colorful paintings from the Bible, like I remember it. I begin down the aisle, Rosi. This time I am alone. But it is the same aisle, the same pews, the same church. I am not the same, and Raquel is not the same.

Charlie was young and nervous that night. He was tall, with light hair and blue eyes, in a white tuxedo. And he shifted from foot to foot. And I remember the argument we had, Rosi, the night Charlie came over and asked for our blessings. "Raquel loves him," you said. "And that's what matters."

"All that matters is what Raquel wants," I said. "That's all that ever matters. But what about our family? Why is that not important?"

"You left your family in Mexico, remember? This is your new family, get used to it."

Charlie read her a poem, they said their vows, Father Thomas blessed them, and I had a gringo son-in-law who called me by my first name.

Later, little Juan Armijo stepped in front of the band to sing "Sabor a Mí," and I took you in my arms and you moved with such grace, and everyone stopped to watch. Maybe we couldn't talk too much, especially then, but did that matter when the music started? Tell me, Rosi, weren't we talking then, as we danced, did you not love me then?

"Tanto tiempo disfrutamos de este amor," I sing to myself. *"Nuestras almas se acercaron tanto asi."*

I stop and sit in a pew and think I should pray. I do not know why. What do I ask for? I have asked for so much. Maybe God gives only to those who ask for nothing. I get on my knees, and I ask one more time for forgiveness. Please forgive my indiscretions, Dear Lord. I was young and foolish. But I always loved my Rosi. Please bring her back to me, please let me hear her voice.

Back in the car Peter sits like a stone, staring at the church. I climb in and close the door and expect him to say something. The keys hang in the ignition, waiting for him to turn them. But his hands are in his lap, and he is staring down for a long time. Then he looks up at the church. His eyes are shiny. He sniffs and says, "There was something wrong with my son's kidneys, Juan. He had end-stage renal disease. They didn't know what it was exactly, they never found out what was wrong, just the kidneys, they weren't filtering the blood properly." He leans back and takes in a breath. "We had him on dialysis, but that wasn't working. He was getting sick all the time, and they told us that he needed a transplant. My wife, Sharon, well she's diabetic, so she says to me that I need to donate my kidney. But here's the thing, for some reason, I don't know, I hesitated. I flinched. And she saw it, my wife, she caught me. I didn't just step up to the plate."

The church bells begin chiming. The people around the church start cleaning up. Men climb down from the ladders.

Peter wipes his eyes with the back of his hand.

I clear my throat. There is so much sadness, I do not know what to tell him. The bell stops ringing, and I say, "We have all done bad things."

Peter looks at me and nods. He sits up and takes in a long breath. "Yeah," he says.

"What happened to your boy?" I ask.

"Tyler? Well, he's doing fine, actually. That's the funny thing, his little brother happened to be a much better match, and it all worked out okay in the end. But Sharon and I know the truth. And that's why she left me, and that's why I'm out here. New Mexico is a long way from Cincinnati."

"It is a long way from Chihuahua too. We are both a long way from home."

Peter wipes his eyes again and looks at me. "Chihuahua? Is that where you're from? That's the place where the dog comes from, right? The little dog?"

Peter turns the key, and the car starts. He pulls the car out of the parking lot onto the main road and says, "Yeah, those dogs, I don't know, they're always shivering, aren't they? They must be cold or something. Maybe they're scared."

On the road into Taos he talks about his boys, Tyler and Evan, how Tyler was an accident and was always sick with something. "Evan has always looked out for his big brother, taking care of him and whatnot," he says. "Hell, Sharon's right, they don't need me or my lousy paycheck. Selling fire alarms doesn't get your kids into private school, I'll tell you that much. But they'll be just fine without me. Better, probably."

"You are a weak man," I tell him. "You are weak because you would rather drive a car than do what you know you should do."

"I'm sorry," he says. "I didn't catch that. What'd you say?"

"Your family is more important than your pity."

"Let me think about that for a minute." He is quiet, then he says, "Damn, you're like a sage or something, Juan. See, I knew I picked up the right guy. You're right, you're totally right, pity sucks. I hate people who feel sorry for themselves."

We drive into town, past markets, restaurants, the post office.

He says, "Time has gotten away from us a little bit. I'm sorry about that. What is that address again?"

I pull out the card and show it to him.

"Arroyo Seco?" he says. "I thought you said Taos?"

"It is near Taos. Just past."

Peter stops into a gas station and takes the card with him as he gets out of the car. When he comes back, he says, "Okay, no problem. There are directions on the back of this, you know. It tells you how to get there." He looks at the card and says, "Are you sure you're going to a funeral?"

As we drive through Taos, past art galleries and restaurants, Peter tells me that this is where he'll be staying for the next few days. "I'm going to look at some art, do some exploring, see the Rio Grande. Maybe I'll take off my clothes and sit in one of those hot springs I heard about down by the river."

The sun is slipping down into the canyon, and big red clouds are moving in. It is now past seven, and Peter is driving fast. He pulls off the main road and starts heading toward the mountains. We drive through a small town, Arroyo Seco, past a bar with people outside, drinking beer. The road comes to a fork and Peter stops. "This is where we go on the dirt road, I think," he says. "The road less traveled." His little car shakes and bounces. "You're wearing a ring there, Juan. Are you married?"

"Yes," I say. "I was. She is dead."

"Oh, I'm sorry to hear that."

"I have two children, Mario and Raquel. My first two boys died many years ago."

"You would have given your kidneys for them, wouldn't you?"

"Quit it," I tell him. "You are not the first man to act without courage."

Out the window horses eat grass in the dusty red light. They stand like shadows, dark ghosts in the falling sun.

"It's something out here, isn't it?" he says. "I could see just escaping out here. Chucking it all and hiding out here."

"That's what you are doing," I say.

He thinks for a moment, and then says, "You know what? You're right. About everything." He turns the wheel, and we are going down a long, gravel driveway with cars parked along the sides. "I've been running away for a long time," he says.

"Listen," I tell him. "Get some sleep, then go back to your wife and tell her she married a coward. But you have found strength in your heart. Being alone is no good, Peter. In the short time, yes, it may be good, but in the long time you get lonely and for that you may as well be dead."

He pulls up to a large adobe house. "Strange place for a funeral," he says.

"There is no funeral," I say. "My daughter is getting married."

"I know, I read the invitation," he says. "Congratulations. But why did you tell me she died?"

"She is marrying a woman."

"Oh," he says. "She threw you a curveball, huh?"

I get out of the car. "Thank you for the ride, Peter."

"Take care, Juan. It was a pleasure." I close the door, and he sits in the car and watches me as I walk up to the house. He honks his horn and then drives away. Dust rises off the ground and floats in the air.

I knock on the door. There are music and voices from somewhere on the other side of the house. I knock again, but no one answers. The dust is now settling on the road behind me, and it is getting dark. Big purple clouds fill the sky.

I walk around the house and music gets louder. There is a stack of wood, piñon logs, and a rusty ax lying on the ground. There is a hole in the ground and a mound of dry, sandy dirt and a shovel leaning up against the house. Beside the hole, there is a bush in a clay pot, waiting to be planted.

The music gets louder with people shouting and laughter.

Through shrubs and around a shed, I move, and down below

me on a patio of red tile, people are dancing and clapping their hands. The lights from the house shine down on them. They are mostly gringos trying to salsa, smiling, swiveling their hips. Raquel is dancing with the short-haired woman from the photo. Raquel's hair is pulled back. Her deep, dark eyes and those full lips and her cheekbones, sharp like a statue, remind me of you, Rosalinda.

The valley below fills with dark gray and pink clouds, and the wind pushes the branches of the trees. The bushes around me shake. The song ends and the gringos clap their hands. Some are on the side with drinks in their hands talking English to each other. Raquel's children, Stephen and Elizabeth, adults now, stand by their father, Charlie, Raquel's ex-husband. What is he doing here, Rosi? This is like no wedding I have been to. It is a small party with a few friends.

Raquel puts her hand up and moves away from the group, saying something to a young man at a wooden table, where the music comes from. Voices can be heard, people talking. Raquel comes back to the woman with the short hair and says something to the other people. They smile and nod and step back, leaving the dance floor for the two women. And then trumpets fill the air. Do you hear that? Those trumpets and that rhythm, that slow rhythm that you loved so much?

Raquel holds up her hand. A man's voice sings out, *"Tanto tiempo disfrutamos de este amor,"* and the woman takes Raquel in her arms, and they begin to dance. *"Si negaras mi presencia en tu vivir."* She moves like soft wind, and her eyes show only happiness as she spins away from the woman. The man sings those words, those familiar words, Rosi, remember? I sing them out as the woman takes Raquel's hand and brings her back. *"Tanta vida yo te di."* I want to tell her what the words mean—*I gave you so much life*. If she only knew the language. *I do not pretend to be your owner*, the man sings. *I am not in control*. She turns away and then spins back into the woman's arms with such ease that I cannot contain myself. It is like I am dancing with you again, Rosi, the way your fingers touched my palm, with your thumb on my wrist and the wrinkle on your cheek when you smiled. I release you and spin around, with my arms out like a child, and then I pull you close to me, my hand moving from your hip to your back, my lips at the top of your ear.

But then the song ends, and Raquel steps back and says something, and then she puts her arms around the woman and they hold each other. There is clapping, and then the thick clouds above us start to send down rain.

"Did you feel that?" Raquel says. "It's raining!"

A flamenco starts up. Raquel turns and snaps her fingers at her ex-husband, Charlie, who walks out and starts dancing. Stephen comes out and dances with his arms in the air. The short-haired woman turns and dances with our granddaughter, Elizabeth. Raindrops come down bigger and bigger, sending down those who have come before. More and more people come out, shouting and clapping. They crowd together, smiling as they dance in the rain, and laughing, these people I'll never know with people I've known forever.

Reception

After he quit that exterminating job, Uncle Cliff started his own business picking up roadkill. Sometimes he took me along. On the CB voices buzzed and crackled. If a report came over about a dead deer on the roadside, Uncle Cliff put on his hazards and pushed on the gas. Sometimes it was a baby doe with legs as thin as sticks, and other times it was a buck with a full rack on his head. One day Uncle Cliff and me got eight deer and drove them down to the Buck and Bass. Larson, a Vietnam vet, an ex-pro wrestler, and other things just as interesting, ran a butcher shop out the back of the store. He cut the deer into steaks and sent them to fancy restaurants in D.C. and New York and Atlanta. On average, Uncle Cliff made one hundred dollars per deer. Some days that would mean a thousand dollars, others zero. It was enough to keep us afloat anyhow.

Papa hadn't worked for a while on account of the dizzy spells and seizures that pushed his eyeballs back in his head. His back arched and he flipped around so much Uncle Cliff started referring to it in fishing terms, as if Papa was a smallmouth bass bouncing around the bottom of a boat. Papa needed to sleep awhile and then he smiled a lot and he even looked at me without a scowl. And he didn't complain so much about the TV, which didn't get NBC unless the front door was open. In winter the house got awful cold when *Columbo* came on, or *McCloud*, or *The Rockford Files*. The summer it filled up with bugs because of baseball and *Adam 12*. That summer we got bit up so bad Uncle Cliff and me went out to the swamp off of Chicken Bridge Road and captured us some toads and put them in every corner of the house with a fresh bowl of water besides.

One day I was up on the roof making animals out of clouds when I saw Mrs. Castagna out at her mailbox opening an envelope and reading a letter. She took a long time, and when she finished she stepped out into the road and read the letter again, and then she turned and stuffed the letter back into the envelope and threw it into the mailbox. What happened next was like nothing I'd ever seen. Mrs. Castagna slammed that mailbox shut, ripped it off the post, and threw it into the road. It skipped on the gravel and ended up in the ditch. Then she got in her car and flew out of the driveway, the tires spinning, sending rocks and dust over the dented mailbox.

She was long gone by the time I read the letter. I sat in the ditch, below the road, waving gnats out of my face. The letter was from Mr. Castagna, the man who was never around anymore. He used to work in the meatpacking plant, until he lost three fingers being careless with the overtime, Mr. Reese said. The letter was from Memphis. Mr. Castagna wrote he'd found work on a garbage barge on the Mississippi and he wouldn't be back. He wished her God's blessings and told her not to wait around.

When I got up and carried the mailbox back to the post, the sky was mostly clear and the hot summer sun was pushing down on my shoulders. I ran home and got a hammer and some nails. I knew how to repair mailboxes. After it was secure I wrote a little note that said, "Saw your mailbox and thought I'd try to help it along." I didn't sign it. That would add to the mystery.

This was my thinking: a failed romance is an open door, a door Papa for sure wouldn't walk through, but maybe with some help, he might allow himself to get shoved through. Besides, Papa and Mrs. Castagna always got along. There was that time my friend Avery James and me dropped eggs down the Castagnas' chimney, but besides that they were always cordial. After they first met I remember Papa saying to Mama, "She's all right, for a Yankee."

Mrs. Castagna reminded me of my mama, a woman with temper, a certain orneriness about her that frightens off some men. But not Papa. He wanted a little kick.

Papa and Mama were always getting in fights and making up, getting all smootchy on the sofa. One time Papa made Mama so mad she killed Louis, Papa's pet rooster, and gutted him and stuffed him and set him on the fence. Next morning when Papa slept in, he said, "I wonder what happened to Louis this morning." He looked out the back window, and there was Louis standing so erect and proud, his crimson feathers shining in the sunlight.

The next day when Papa picked Louis up off the ground after a windy night, he held him close to his chest and stroked his head. He came in the house and didn't say a thing. Mama didn't look at him. She was in her robe, flipping bacon on the griddle. Papa went into his bedroom and shut the door.

To this day Louis stands on the dresser watching over Papa while he sleeps. That stuffed bird is a reminder of my mama, and something we never talked about, because, in a way, Papa thought she died on account of me, though he never said nothing about it. After her passing, Papa turned to the television and stopped eating with me.

What happened was my mama died in an ice storm. She was out back in the shed for some reason. It was morning. The day before, we'd had some snow and ice and Papa told me to shovel every step and walkway. So I did it, all but the steps to the shed, and then I took off sledding with Avery and Jack. So then Mama slipped and hit her head and broke her hip. But that isn't what did it, not really. Another storm moved through, and by that afternoon Mama was covered.

That night when Mama still hadn't showed up, Papa called around town and nobody had seen her. He called the sheriffs and filed a report, and then got sick and put his head in the toilet. Two days later the ice and snow began to melt.

Word got around that Mrs. Castagna was going to become Ms. Castagna, that by the end of summer, the divorce papers would be signed and she'd be made available to such men as Thornton Wiles, Linford Johnson, and Raymond Mosley, the three bachelors of Frostburg, North Carolina. Uncle Cliff wasn't in the running. People had been talking, whispering, about him not having a date for fifteen years and not even looking at pretty girls.

And nobody even talked about Papa being available. They felt sorry for him, a widower with some kind of sickness most people didn't know nothing about. So, according to everyone, Papa didn't even have a chance. I was going to change that. Mrs.

Castagna may have been a Yankee, but she wasn't ugly, and just maybe she'd get Papa to talk to me again.

When Uncle Cliff came in after the firework display down at Colonel Ford Park, he looked out of sorts. "What the hell you doing, Treat?" He shuffled sideways and fell onto the couch.

"Nothing," I said. Papa had had an attack, first one in months, right after the fireworks. I was up on the roof watching the clear sky fill up with the colored lights, and just after the grand finale that Timmy "Digger" Graves is so famous for around here, the house started shaking, and it had that peculiar rhythm of Papa's sickness. I jumped down and got into the kitchen in time to move a chair out of the way. A few minutes later it stopped, and I got the tape measure and stretched it out along his arms and legs. That's when Uncle Cliff stumbled in.

"They don't know nothing," he slurred. "What do they know? Goddamned rednecks." His body slipped down the sofa and went limp. Papa's head moved, and then he looked up at me. His eyes were empty and still.

The divorce papers came earlier than expected. By the middle of August, Mrs. Castagna was single. But most of the town didn't hold her responsible. She was simply a victim of bad judgment that's common in Northerners. Jimmy Castagna, a local boy whose New Jersey ancestors came down after the Civil War to exploit us Southerners, was never any good. That's what people will tell you. He lost the family fortune—a textile plant down on the Haw River—by the age of thirty and had to go up north to find anybody who'd take his hand in marriage. They'd only been married a few years before he lost his fingers and moved away.

Up on the roof I put together my plan. I still had to get Papa a suit. But I had no money, and I couldn't ask Uncle Cliff on account of him trying to talk me out of it. But I knew Papa's size, so half the job was done. I'd been going around town recently looking at men's shoulders and bellies, surprised, I guess, by all the variations. I couldn't find anybody who was just kind of normal, like Papa. I was ready to give up and figure out a way to earn money so as I could buy him a suit down at the PTA Thrift Shop. But as I stood there I saw old Mr. Owens leaving his trailer. He was wearing one of his fancy three-piece suits, probably on his way to the Christian Science church in Rocky Mount. As he got in his car I noticed that he was about the same size as Papa. His shoulders were rounder, maybe, and he was taller. But he was close anyway, closer than the other men in town. The only way to know if he was the right one, the only way to know for sure was to get down off the roof and find my way into his trailer, which wasn't too hard on account of two strands of wire Avery James showed me how to use.

I measured a suit right there on Mr. Owen's bed. His legs were a little longer, and the sleeves on the jacket needed to be trimmed an inch, but besides that Papa had himself what looked like a good fit. Mr. Owens had a whole closet of fancy suits, so many I didn't know how to choose. The one I picked was like the one Columbo would wear. It was a light brown two-piece thing. I grabbed a white shirt and a tie and I ran out of there so fast I don't know if I locked the door behind me or not.

My first job was done. Now I had to write the note. I sat up on the roof that night and looked to the stars for inspiration.

Dear Ms. Castagna,

Please accept my condolences. I know how it feels to lose a loved one. If you ever want to chat, I'm right down the road.

Conrad Hopkins

The next day I set the note in Ms. Castagna's mailbox with a blooming lily I'd yanked out of Mrs. Graves's garden. That afternoon I sat on the roof and watched her as she read the note. She held the flower up to her nose and then turned and started walking down the road towards our house. It was hot and thick, and as she walked she wiped her forehead with the back of her hand. I didn't expect this, not today. The house was a mess, and the toads were hopping all around, on the furniture and everything.

Her feet scraped along the gravel some more until she was facing the front of our house. I peeked around the chimney at her standing there. She stared at the front porch and smelled the flower again, and then she turned and started up the road, back where she came from.

That night after Papa went to sleep, I cleaned the house, scrubbing the floors and the walls, everything Mama used to do. It was the toads that took so long. I got a box from under the house and started filling it up. I hadn't realized how many there were. When you live with something you just get used to it, I guess.

Uncle Cliff barged in and flopped down on the sofa. "Hey, Treat," he said. "What are you doing?"

"Nothing," I said.

"Getting rid of future kings?" He got up and stumbled to the middle of the room and nudged the box with his foot. I was under the kitchen table, cupping my hands around one when he said, "I got news for you frogs. You'll never make it. It's just a fairy tale!" He pulled the lid off the box and lifted one out. He brought the toad up close and looked him in the eyes. He had a look on his face as he stared at that toad, almost like he was about to cry. He brought the toad up closer and kissed it.

"See?" he said. "See?" He swayed a little bit and sucked in air. "It's just a fairy tale." Uncle Cliff's eyes started filling with tears. "It ain't true. None of it."

I wanted to tell Uncle Cliff that it was supposed to be a princess that kisses the toad, but I knew that would only make things worse.

He dropped the toad in the box and flopped back onto the couch. "They can say what they want." He closed his eyes and lay down. "They don't know nothing," he mumbled. "Nothing."

I took the box outside and walked into the dark woods. It was so dark I had to feel my way from tree to tree. When I got back Uncle Cliff was curled up on the sofa and the house was still. It was as quiet and clean as it had ever been. I climbed onto the roof and under the beam of my flashlight, I composed another note.

Dear Ms. Castagna,

It sure is a pretty time of year, don't you think? When the sun goes down, the sky looks like a painting. It would sure be nice to sit out on the porch with a cool glass of tea and look at the sky, maybe chat about things. I've got so much tea I don't know what to do with. I hope you are doing well.

Sincerely,
Conrad Hopkins

The next morning I put three big jars of tea on the roof to sit in the sun all day. Then I went over to Mrs. Graves's and yanked another lily and put it on the note in Ms. Castagna's mailbox. But as I was setting it in there, wouldn't you know it but Mrs. Castagna peeled around the corner, the way she always did, and caught me dead to rights. So what did I do? I slammed the box shut and sprinted like a ground squirrel through the hedge and into the woods. I stopped for a second and listened as she got out of her car and went to the mailbox. "Treat!" she said.

I knew just by the sound of her voice that I'd failed. Like Uncle Cliff says, "It doesn't take a rap on the head to kill a fish." The world has a harshness all its own, and it reminds you with nudges and whispers.

Later that night I was looking at some pictures of Papa in his younger days. He was a handsome man with a strong chin and a full mustache that was a touch redder than his blond hair, and in the pictures he looked good, standing next to Mama, or holding a smallmouth, or repairing the Plymouth with grease on his face. When his hair was combed and he stood up straight, with the right clothes on, Papa was, as they said in town, impressive looking. And standing in the door that night, staring at Mrs. Castagna, the color rushed back into his cheeks and he looked instantly younger.

"Pardon me?" he said, taking off his baseball cap.

"I said I'd love some iced tea, Mr. Hopkins." She was standing under the porch light in a sleeveless yellow summer dress, and the tan skin on her shoulders gleamed.

Papa straightened his hair and said, "Mrs. Castagna." He looked back at me confused.

I didn't know what to say, so I poured some iced tea and shouted from the kitchen, "My Papa makes the best iced tea in Eason County, Ms. Castagna." I put a glass in Papa's hand and said, "Sure is a nice night to sit on the porch and chat awhile."

"Sure is," Ms. Castagna said.

Papa was looking at me all crazy. "Mrs. Castagna, you must forgive me," he said.

"Papa," I said, "the porch swing is all cleaned off, and there ain't many gnats or nothing."

"Isn't," he corrected. "We don't use ain't in this house."

This was news to me.

Papa sighed and said, "I guess it is a pretty night."

Ms. Castagna smiled and took a step back as Papa went out onto the porch. "Well, I'll be," he said. "Sure does feel good out here." He handed me his cap and shut the door in my face.

I climbed up on the roof and scooted down the front on my stomach. The porch swing was creaking a bit, and then there was a long batch of silence.

"Sure is good tea," Ms. Castagna said.

"Oh, I gotta be honest with you, Mrs. Castagna, my son made it."

"It's just the right sweetness."

"Margaret showed him how, I guess, before she passed."

"I suppose you heard about Jimmy," she said.

"In this town?" he said. They both chuckled. "I hate to sound this way, Mrs. Castagna . . ."

"Frances, please," she said.

"Frances."

"Or Franny," she said. "My friends up north, they call me Franny. Or Fran. Whatever you like."

"Okay."

"What were you going to say?"

"I don't know," he said. "Would you believe it? I forgot. I forgot what I was going to say."

He sounded normal. It had been a long time since I'd heard him sound like a regular person, like one of the old men who sit around the barrel down at the Buck and Bass, just talking.

"Oh, yeah, that's it," he said. "Now I remember. I wanted to ask you how you ever ended up with Jimmy. I mean, forgive me for saying so, but I always thought you deserved better."

"I thought I knew him," she said. "You know how that is. He told me he would one day own a textile mill. That's about how long he owned it, too. But he was so nice and he had manners, you know, not like the people I hung out with up north. He held the door for me and pulled out chairs." It was quiet for a minute and then she said, "But it's easy to fall in love when you're young."

"That's for sure," Papa said.

"But I don't want to talk about him. There's so much more to talk about in the world."

"Can I ask you something?" Papa said. "Why didn't you move back north when all this started happening?"

"I still might," she said. "I haven't made up my mind yet. But I've made it my home here, sort of. I know everybody."

"Which ain't always so great," Papa said.

"You can say that again. People talk and talk, about everybody. But that's no different than anywhere else. I'm telling you, up in New York and Jersey, people's traps are always running."

"I'm sure you've heard about me," Papa said.

"Well you're my neighbor," she said. "I know you. I don't listen to what everyone says. But is it true you brought home some medals from the war?"

"I wouldn't call a Purple Heart a medal," he said. "I mean, I just got wounded is all."

"You're being modest. But we don't have to talk about it if you don't want to."

It was quiet again, and then the swing creaked a bit.

"You know why I'm here, don't you?" she said. "I know it seems pushy of me. But I got this note in my mailbox, and I was hoping it was from you, but it sure doesn't look like a man's handwriting."

Paper crinkled and then there was silence.

"There was a flower with it," she said. "Mrs. Graves saw Treat the other day pulling lilies out of her garden. She didn't say anything to him because, as she said, to see a boy in a flower garden is so nice she didn't want to spoil it."

I couldn't believe it. Why did she have to say anything? Is that the way Yankees do things? Just talk and talk until it's all ruined?

"Okay," she said. "So I know it's not from you. So what? And I know it's forward, but my motto is 'If you aren't forward, you're backward.' So here I am. If you want me to go home, I understand."

"Treat wrote this?" I could tell Papa was mad. I could see him in my mind, his jaw muscles working as he clenched his teeth.

"I saw him putting it in my mailbox today. And there was a lily with it, just blooming."

Suddenly I didn't like Ms. Castagna anymore.

"Truth be told," Papa said, and then he chuckled, "I was a little confused when I saw you standing at the door. And at first I thought it a bit forward, but it's nice talking, I guess."

"There's nothing wrong with talking. Except the kind they do in town. I'm the hot topic, you know. You used to be it, when

Marge passed on, bless her soul. Now I am. I heard people are taking bets on whether or not I'm going to stay."

"I'm sorry I didn't think of it myself," he said.

"Excuse me?"

"The note," he said. "The flowers."

"Oh," she said. "It's a nice night, isn't it?"

"It sure is," Papa said.

Where'd his anger go? I was up there, just a few feet above them, in shock.

They talked and talked, and by the time she left, Ms. Castagna managed to talk Papa into taking her to the Hog Days Dance down at Brody's Barn behind the Baptist church. Stewart Bush's Good Time Cavaliers were going to be filling the barn with the best hillbilly music this side of the Appalachians. Ms. Castagna roped him into it by saying, "Can you imagine what those people in town would say to that? All bets out the window! Think about it, the sick widower doing the two-step with the crazy divorced Yankee. Imagine the looks on their faces!"

Ms. Castagna seemed excited as Papa escorted her off the porch and up the road. I stood up and watched them as they walked in the moonlight, their shadows spreading out behind them, the gravel crunching beneath their feet.

The next morning I carried Mr. Owens's suit out and set it on the sofa beside Papa, who was sitting there reading the paper.

"What the hell?" he said.

"Try it on," I said. "See if it fits. Dance is tomorrow."

Just then Uncle Cliff came out of his room in his underpants. "Hm," he said, scratching his messy head. "What's that?"

Papa exploded. "What's it look like, Cliff? Haven't you got any eyes in your damn head? It's a suit!" He stood up. "It's a god-damned suit!" he yelled. "Haven't you ever seen a suit before?" He went into his bedroom and slammed the door.

"What the hell was that?" Uncle Cliff said. "You gettin' on his nerves, Treat? Huh?"

"I don't know."

"Well," he said, "Keep it up. Someone needs to get on his nerves, give a shock to his system. Hey, is this the suit you were working on?" He bent over and fingered the fabric. "That's a nice-lookin' weave."

A few minutes later Papa came out of his room wearing a dark brown, plaid thing that was so tight in the pants I actually felt uncomfortable just looking at him.

"Now what in sam hell?" Uncle Cliff said. "What's wrong with this one?" He pointed to the suit on the sofa.

"That's not my suit," Papa said. "This here is my suit."

"A suit, by definition, is supposed to suit you, Connie," Uncle Cliff said. "Now all you're going to get from wearing that is a lawsuit." Uncle Cliff flopped back on the sofa bursting with laughter. "A lawsuit," he said again. "Get it?"

Papa wanted to say something so bad his face turned red. But then I realized it was probably just the pants squeezing all the blood from his legs into the upper region of his body.

From high up in the loft, Brody's Barn looked as big as the high school gymnasium. Avery James and me sat up there watching Stewart Bush's Good Time Cavaliers begin the evening with "Goodbye Savannah." Mr. and Mrs. Casey were the first couple on the dance floor. Most everyone else was standing around chatting. Papa and Ms. Castagna showed up halfway through the song and started talking to Thornton Wiles and his date, Ms. Camden, the grade school teacher over at Eastbrooke Elementary. When the song ended everybody clapped. From up in the loft, it sounded like a bunch of firecrackers popping on the dance floor. I noticed people staring at Papa and Ms. Castagna, and I knew what they were saying.

When the Good Time Cavaliers broke into a hopping version of "The Blue Ridge Country Down," Ms. Castagna pulled Papa out onto the dance floor, and he grabbed her and twirled her around maybe the way a drunken, clumsy Gene Kelly might. But at least in Mr. Owens's suit he could move around the dance floor without causing a ruckus.

A little later in the evening Mr. Owens came in the barn with an old lady I had never seen before. They went over to the punch bowl and chatted with Mr. and Mrs. Carruthers. I hadn't thought of the possibility of Mr. Owens showing up.

Later, when I got home, Uncle Cliff was sitting up on the roof with a six-pack between his legs. He was blowing on his harmonica. He'd started to learn songs, melodies that made sense, not that rambling stuff he used to do, but things that stuck in your head, things you hummed in the tub the next day. "How's things, pard?" he asked.

"All right. What's that you're playing?"

"Oh, that? Don't know, just made it up. Pretty, though, isn't it? I like this part." He blew for a while and then stopped and said, "I think I'll call it 'A Great Sadness and a Great Happiness.' What do you think?"

He played it again. The notes drifted out into the darkness, moving slowly and dissolving in the trees. I lay back and looked at the sky. "I snuck into to the Hog Days Dance," I said.

"Hm." Uncle Cliff took the harmonica away from his mouth and swigged on a beer.

"Papa and Ms. Castagna were dancing."

"That's what you do at a dance, Treat."

"Yeah," I said. "He let on like he didn't want to go. But I think he did."

"Of course he did," Uncle Cliff said. "Loneliness will make a man do just about anything. No disrespect to her. She is a nice lady and all." He blew on his harmonica some more and then stopped and looked at me. "I've been watching you, Treat," he said. "I know which way the wind blows. And I've been up here thinkin' about things. You know, our dad, your grampa, well, when he got mad, he just pretended you weren't there, he made you invisible, just like my brother is doing to you. It's sad, is what it is. It's a sad, sad thing."

He drank some beer, and then looked off into the distance. "You know, Connie loved your mother like I couldn't believe, and when he came back from the war, he just had to be by her, all the time, he couldn't be alone. She was a spitfire, your mother, and she'd get him riled up and then she'd make him laugh, and everything. You remember. And I guess what I'm gettin' at, Treat, is that we get happy in this life, and we get sad, and accidents happen. They happen. And it don't do any good to blame anybody."

He started blowing on his harmonica. I listened for a while, and I knew what he was saying. But I still wished I could've gone back to that morning with the snow shovel in my hand and Avery and Jack standing there with trash can lids, begging me to take off to Cutter's Hill where the sledding was so fast your ears froze off. I wished I could've gone back just to shovel those last few steps at the shed, just clear them off, make them safe.

"It's okay, Treat," Uncle Cliff said, touching my shoulder. "It's all right." He put his arm around me and pulled me to him, and we sat there for a long while. And then he took a sip of his beer and said, "Listen, them toads are still hanging around. I don't think you got them all. I saw one under the kitchen sink. And one of them was floating in the commode. You got any ideas on how we can fix this? You know how we could get a hold of a snake or something?"

"School starts next week," I said. "And Mr. Rondell has a boa constrictor in his biology class. I could get my hands on that, I bet."

Uncle Cliff blew on his harmonica, and I lay back and looked up at the sky again. It's better to look up than down. As Mama used to say, "Where you spend most of your time looking is where you're destined to end up." Some clouds moved slowly through the sky, spreading a thin veil over the stars.

Papa's Plymouth pulled up front of Ms. Castagna's place. He got out and walked her to her door. I couldn't see her porch from where I stood, so I don't know if it was a handshake or something more.

"What is it?" Uncle Cliff said.

"Papa's home," I said.

By the time Papa was getting in his car, Uncle Cliff had stood up and said, "I guess we better see how it went, huh?" He slid his harmonica in his pocket, grabbed his beer, and climbed down.

Papa pulled up in front of the house, got out of the car and jogged up the steps. Just then I realized that the television hadn't been on for hours. No baseball or *Adam 12*. Papa moved through the house now like a young man. I could feel it vibrating beneath me.

A car with rectangular headlights pulled into the driveway. Mr. Owens got out and left the door hanging open, the inside of the car all lit up. He came onto the porch and cleared his throat.

After several knocks, the screen door creaked on its hinges, and what I heard was this:

"Mr. Hopkins?"

"Oh, hello, Mr. Owens."

"I hate to bother you."

"No, not at all."

"I just noticed, after bumping into you on the dance floor, that your suit is familiar to me."

"Is that so?"

"And forgive me, Mr. Hopkins, may I ask you where you got it?"

"Well, I don't know actually. It was a gift."

"Hm."

"Is there a problem, Mr. Owens?"

"Well, if you must know, I have, or should say, had a suit just like it. But one day I lost it."

"How does a man lose a suit?"

"Well, how shall I say this?" Mr. Owens said. "I came home and it was gone. And well, when I saw you tonight, I just wondered where you got it, because I've been looking but haven't found one like it anywhere, you understand, to replace it."

"Hm."

"I just don't know who would come into a man's house and steal his suit."

"Oh, I do," my father said. "You better believe it, Mr. Owens. I know who stole your suit."

"Mr. Hopkins?"

"I'm sorry, Mr. Owens. Believe me, I'm sorry," Papa said. He moved across the porch, the screen door slammed shut, and his feet pounded down the steps. "Treat!"

He hadn't said my name in months.

"Treat!"

Mama told me he'd come up with the name the day I was born because even though I'd been an accident he wanted to always think of me as special, as a treat. Now as he moved out into the dark shadows, I stood victorious on the rooftop, the sky sparkling above me.

"Treat!" he shouted, "So help me God!"

It is now October and leaves are burning. The other day Papa, Uncle Cliff, Timmy Graves, and me helped Ms. Castagna and her brother Tony load all her stuff into a big truck. There's a For Sale sign in front of her house.

Papa was acting like he didn't care. But he was philosophizing more than usual, talking about life as the truck pulled away.

I spent every weekend in September digging up Mr. Owens's mossy yard so he could plant some fescue, have a proper lawn. "Who needs a rototiller," Papa said to Mr. Owens, "when you got Treat here?"

"It's looking good," Mr. Owens said.

his was supposed to be my big lesson for stealing the suit. "If
ke an inch," Papa said, "you gotta give back a mile."

The first week of September, Uncle Cliff started talking about
going to technical college to take a class in antique furniture
repair. "I can't spend the rest of my life picking up dead deer," he
said. "As much as I enjoy it, well, there's just no future in it."

Papa got some medicine to help with the seizures, and he got
himself a job. He starts next week down at Wallace Appliance, selling washers and dryers. Occasionally we eat dinner together, at the
table with the TV off, some baked beans and meatloaf or something. Mama's chair we leave empty, and we stay quiet, imagining,
I guess, what the conversation might be like if she was still here.
Sometimes he'll say something about somebody in town, or he'll
ask me how my day was, how school is going, if I like my teacher.
But usually we just eat.

The other day Uncle Cliff told me Papa is going to go pick up
an antenna so now we can look forward to a warm winter and better reception.

And about that snake, Ulysses is his name. He sure did a number on them toads. We haven't seen a toad in weeks. Trouble is,
we haven't seen Ulysses either. So if you come by and you happen
upon a six-foot boa constrictor, don't be alarmed. He's harmless.
Just let me know where he is, because Mr. Rondell is offering a
twenty-five dollar reward.

Ruby

My father refuses to put Ruby to sleep.

"Please," he says from the other side of the door. "Go away."

"It's mercy," I say, pulling the *Do Not Disturb* sign from the doorknob. "Do you want her to suffer?"

A twisted stench comes from under the door. Behind me, cars roar past the Almost Home Motel sign, the word *Vacancy* lit up under a blue sky. *Weekly Rates. Cable TV.*

I go home and call my brother, Stevie, up in Eugene.

"I got my shotgun," Stevie says. "It's loaded. And I got a shovel. That would do the trick."

"Come on, Stevie."

"You know, Sis," he says, "I haven't killed anything in a while."

Ruby is a toothless, stocky pitbull mix who has lost most of her hair and leaves piles of dander everywhere she goes. She also has a lump the size of a softball sticking out of her side, and she pees and craps all over the place. My father found her a while back, out at the firewood lot where he used to work part-time under the table. As the splitting machine quartered a fir tree, she came up to him and begged for the bologna sandwich he was eating. "The lump was only the size of a thumb then," he once said, sticking up his thumb. "Yeah, about like that."

Mrs. Nasarinskia calls for the fifth time in two days. "Your fawdder has to vacate de premises now or I call de police."

"Mrs. Nasarinskia," I say. "Please give me time."

"Time is not mine to give."

"Me and my brother are going to take care of the dog today."

"Dis a respectable motel. All maids speak English!"

The sun is breaking through the clouds, which doesn't happen often around here. When the sun shines, everything speeds up. If things were different I would turn on the radio and clean my apartment. I would call Liza, and we'd go to the park and watch the kids play on the jungle gym. We'd pick out which ones we want to kidnap and call our own.

Liza lives on the reservation. She deals blackjack at the casino and teaches Sunday school. She also has a husband and two kids, and she says she's in love with me. She doesn't have an Indian name, but if she did, she says it would be *Fire Burns Inside*, because, well, she's nice, and sometimes she says romantic things.

• • •

Dad opens the door a crack. Maybe because Stevie is with me now. Dad always responds to Stevie, even though Stevie treats him like shit.

Dad's used-up face hovers behind the chain. The belt of his ratty, light blue terrycloth bathrobe dangles in the small opening. The room is dark behind him, and the TV is on.

"Jesus," Stevie says, stepping back, pinching his nose.

"See?" I say. "Now do you believe me?"

"That dog better be dead," Stevie says. "Daddy, tell me that dog is dead and that's what that smell is."

Dad doesn't answer.

A voice shouts from the TV, "Terrorists crossing the border!"

As my father tells it, he let Ruby stay around the firewood lot a few days, and when nobody claimed her, he put her in his Chevy Luv and drove her back to his apartment, even though pets weren't allowed. He had thoughts of training her as a fighter, using her to make a little extra cash down behind the landfill where the migrants hang out and let their dogs go at it. But when he duct-taped a pillow to his arm and attacked her, she refused to fight. So he kicked her in the ribs a few times, and she lay down on her back and waited for him to finish. "I don't know what it is about that stupid bitch," he said, "but she just won't protect herself, and when she goes soft like that, I just want to kill her."

My father's bondo-covered Chevy Luv sits in the pot-holed parking lot. Piled in the back are broken lawn mowers, weed whackers, ceiling fans, desk lamps, computer printers, VCRs, all the things he was working on before he got evicted from his apartment and had to move in here. A maid's cart stands a few doors down, white towels hanging off it, a vacuum humming in a nearby room.

Stevie looks at his watch. "Dad, I got Charlie in the truck. We drove over an hour to get down here, and he really wants to see his grampa. But if you don't clean yourself up, then I won't let Charlie visit with you."

The door closes.

I look back at Stevie's empty pickup. He's lying. Charlie is probably back home, practicing his clarinet or babysitting his retarded little brother, Mickey.

The door opens and Stevie grabs Dad by the neck and drives his limp body backwards onto the bed, onto the messed up sheets and blankets. His robe hangs open, and his massive scar, his *war wound*, zigzags from the top of his boxer shorts up the middle of his pale belly. His feet, in black loafers, hang off the end of the bed.

Ruby barks and whimpers. Her body is sprawled on the bathroom floor in a pool of urine. Her back legs are covered in diarrhea. She struggles to get up. Her claws scrape on the beat-up linoleum and her body slips and splashes down in her own piss.

I'm on my couch, having a beer. The TV's on, with my thumb on the remote—news, sitcom, commercial, reality, crime drama, pledge drive, public access . . .

Stevie calls, his voice echoey and scratched, his truck rumbling. "It's all taken care of, Sis," he says. "Poor thing didn't put up much of a fight. I just pulled off the highway, she practically crawled into the hole."

"Where?"

"I don't know," he says. "You know that turnoff past Sutter's Bridge? Just around the bend there? I put her in some soft dirt down by the gully."

I try to tell Liza what happened. She's sitting beside me on my couch in the living room. I'm on my fourth beer, or fifth, I don't know. It's late, and I'm drunk. She just got off work. She's got her purple vest on and her name tag that says, *Hi I'm Liza*. Her black hair is pulled back and she reeks of cigarette smoke. I tell her how Stevie wrapped the dog up in a piece of canvas and carried her to the back of his pickup, how I argued with him about taking Ruby to the vet, how he told me all the vets are closed and he wasn't about to pay a hundred dollars anyway for an animal doc to do what he could do in thirty seconds on a dirt lot outside of town. I tell her how pee and shit were all over the motel floor, and how my father buried himself under the blankets and put his head under the pillows, and shook with grief, and how prescription pill bottles were everywhere, in other peoples' names, bottles he had stolen from an Allison Crespin, a William Gaffey, a Thomas Sanderville. I tell her how he would take me for drives when I was a girl, just the two of us alone, and how his voice shook when he told me I was pretty, and how I never did anything, how I just sat there and waited for it to end.

Liza calls her husband and tells him she's working a double at the Casino and won't be home until morning.

I tell her how my father might try to kill himself, and even though I've always wished he would just go ahead and do it, now I hope he doesn't.

She calls the motel. No one answers. She suggests we drive over. "He'll be okay," she says, her voice so steady I don't trust it.

In the distance a neon sign burns red in the dark sky: *Almost Home.* We pull into the parking lot and come to a stop outside my dad's room.

His truck is gone. I knock on the door. It still smells.

"I see what you mean," Liza says.

Mr. Nasarinskia stumbles into the darkened front desk area in black, silky pajamas. "You want room?"

"No, sir," Liza says. "We're looking for the guy who was in room seven."

"Oh," he says. "Son-of-bitch. Yes. He leave."

"Did you kick him out?"

"I should've," he says, scratching his brown, bushy hair. "He come early. Drop off key. Good thing he left, because I was going to knock shit out of him."

"Did he say where he was going?"

"I tell him go to hell. Does that help?"

Early the next morning, the phone rings. It's Stevie. He tells me that Dad showed up at his house late last night, and now he's sleeping on a cot next to the foosball table in the garage. "You know," he says. "I shouldn't have fucking listened to you yesterday. I shoulda just hung up the phone. You're always getting your nose into things. What do you care about Dad for? Ya know, I have a family now, Sis, and I'm doin' pretty good."

Stevie has changed from what he was. Now he wears a welder's mask five days a week. The plastic band pushes down his hair and presses red marks onto his forehead. On the rare sunny day, he drinks a Coors and lies in Mickey's wading pool in the backyard by the swing set.

"Stevie, I'm sorry."

"After he wakes up, I'm kickin' him out. He'll probably show up there later today, knockin' on your door, talkin' all sweet the way he does. But don't open it, Sis. Just keep it locked and act like you're not there. If you open that door, only do it to tell him to go to hell. You got me?"

"Yes."

"And if he asks, don't tell him where Mom is. Cuz he still wants to know. I swear to God if you tell him, I'll kill you."

My mother lives with a man down in Crescent City. Jerry DiNardo. He has his own chicken farm, and he's blind in his left eye from a hunting accident when he was a boy. Jerry has three ex-wives and several kids. I've only been down to visit once.

We were sitting around their living room, watching TV, talking about one of his sons, Travis, who was over in Iraq in "a beat-to-shit Humvee with plywood floors and cardboard doors." And out of the blue Jerry and my mom started in on me, asking when I was going to get married, why wasn't I already married, what's wrong with me?

I wanted to ask them to stop, but instead I told them I was going for a walk.

I went outside and ducked into a chicken coop, and started talking to the birds, scrunched in their cages, all clucking and shrieking.

A minute later, the floorboards creaked as Jerry came up behind me.

"Oh, hi, Jerry."

He stopped and cocked his head a little to the side. "Well, hello," he said.

I moved away from him, down towards the dark end of the chicken coop. "Don't these birds need more room?"

He followed me, and then his hand was on my shoulder. "They're just birds."

I looked at his hand on my shoulder, and up at his crooked teeth and wrinkled forehead.

"It's okay," he said, nice and tender. "It'll be all right."

I couldn't move. I was frozen there, just watching, observing, as he started massaging my shoulder.

From the house, my mother's voice called out, "Jerry! Telephone!"

"I know what's going on with you," Jerry whispered. "You don't have to tell me. I'm not a stupid old rooster."

"Jerry! It's Marty, about the mower!"

He turned from me, clomped down the long chicken coop, and went out. "Okay! Okay! I'm coming! Hold your britches."

I stood alone, still unable to move, letting my breath come back to me. Then, a minute later, or two, I walked out of the coop, and into the house, where I grabbed my purse and told my mother that I forgot I had to be someplace and hurried out to the car and drove away.

I haven't called my mom since.

Liza lies there beside me, her mouth slack, her thin lips running along her capped teeth.

The sun is shining again, but I don't want to get up and do things. I want to ask Liza to leave. I want to tell her we need some time apart. I want to say, "I don't know why, but I'm just not feeling it anymore." I repeat these words in my head, trying to get them to sound right.

I get up and make breakfast—a couple of toaster waffles and some instant coffee. Why did I have to tell her so much? Now everything about her makes me sick.

"What smells so good?" Liza says, leaning against the doorframe.

We drive out to the turnoff past Sutter's Bridge. Liza has her country station playing, and she's stopped talking after taking the hint that I don't want to say anything. She cuts the engine and takes a breath. "So what are we doing here?"

I get out of the car and walk down the slope towards the gully. Patches of tall grass blow sideways in the wind. A brown, foamy stream runs over brown rocks. Trees bend and come back and bend again. It doesn't take long to see where Stevie's shovel disturbed the dirt. I go over and kneel down to the dark, turned-over soil.

Stevie was in a hurry. I can tell, cuz the dog isn't fully buried. One of her paws is sticking out of the dirt. I sit down and grab hold of it.

Liza hikes down to me. "What is that?"

"Ruby. My dad's dog. This is her paw."

"What?"

"This is Ruby."

"That's what we came here for? Listen, I really need to get home," Liza says. "I mean, I can't call him again. I can't keep lying like that."

"Then don't," I say. "Don't tell any more lies."

"You know I can't do that, not yet."

"Why?"

"Because," she says, "you know why."

Three knocks. A long pause. And then three more. I'm at the kitchen table playing solitaire with a deck of cards Liza got from the casino. There are naked women on the cards. After a while the knocking stops and there is a distant sound of a car door slamming shut. I get up and open the door and go out to the parking lot. My father's truck sputters and wheezes and then dies. I wave at him. He climbs out and says, "There's my little treasure!"

I make him dinner. But he doesn't eat much, hunched over the plate, scratching his greasy head and breathing from his mouth. His skin is stretched like a sausage and his fingers shake while he eats. "You know a naut is six thousand seventy-six feet?" he says. And then he's quiet for a while.

I keep my distance. I try to stay busy, doing the dishes, organizing the closet.

"That was on the test," he says later, still sitting at the table. "I got that one right, a naut."

He's talking about the test for the captain's license. The one he failed three times when he was younger, before he gave up.

"You got anything needs fixing?" he asks as he pulls out the hide-a-bed. "A radio, microwave, anything?" Sweat runs down the sides of his face, beads pop up on his forehead.

"That's real pretty picture there," he says, pointing to the painting of a country cottage Liza got at a garage sale for a buck. "Real nice. It makes you think about what it might be like to live in a place like that."

He climbs on the bed, rolls onto his side. He pulls the covers over him, and brings his knees up to his chest and shivers. "A house like that, in the middle of nowhere."

The phone rings. It's Liza from the casino, all that noise behind her, pinging bells, music, people talking. "Are you okay? I've been thinking about you all day. How'd you get home this morning?"

"I walked."

"I'm so sorry. But I really needed to get home."

"Of course."

"I feel terrible. I mean, I know it's hard for you right now."

I hang up the phone.

It's over. She already knows too much.

The phone starts ringing. I'm not going to pick it up because I know that no matter how hard I try, I won't be able to hold it in. I'll tell her everything. The phone rings until the answering machine beeps. And then there is silence. And then the phone starts ringing again. But I'm not going to answer. I'm not talking anymore. I'm not going to tell her anything about my father's pirate games, about his hidden treasure, how his fingers traced his treasure map from jewel to jewel, how he said my eyes shined like emeralds, and how his fingers moved down to my soft little pearls and then down further still, all the way down to what he called his favorite jewel of all. The phone stops ringing.

"They're moving," my father says. "They're moving!" I get up and open the bedroom door. My father is sitting upright in the darkness, talking in his sleep. "Stop them!" he shouts. And then he lies back and rolls onto his side, his lips smacking. "Over there!" he says. "Back, back, back!" He mutters some more and then goes quiet.

Tomorrow morning I'll kick him out. After he gets some sleep. I'll tell him to leave, to disappear. I'll let him take a shower first, make sure he's cleaned up. I'll make him breakfast, some eggs, toast, and coffee, and I'll give him twenty dollars for gas. And then I'll tell him that no matter what happens to him, that even when he's sick and dying, I don't ever want to see him again.

I lie in the darkness and think of Ruby out there tonight. The road is empty and quiet. The stream trickles in the gully below, and the grass and the trees are still. Vultures are probably circling above in the clear sky, their long wings black against the stars, as coyotes dig in the dirt, growling and sniffing. They'll eat her sick body, and then they'll get sick, so sick they have to stumble back into the dark woods, back from wherever they came. And then the vultures will slowly swerve down until they get close enough to realize she's not worth it. Stupid dog. Stupid, stupid girl.

An Artist at Work

Russell Peterson woke in darkness. From somewhere outside, a strange sound, a *shuck, shuck, shuck,* drifted up through the cracked bedroom window. He wondered what the sound was, an animal sifting through the trash? A raccoon, a bear? Was it a shovel? Someone digging up the lawn? He thought about waking Genice, who lay beside him, grinding her teeth. But she would just tell him to relax and go back to sleep. He looked at the clock on the night stand: 12:48. Who would be out at this time of night?

The sound stopped. Peterson rolled out of bed and went to the window. Below, his son was in the middle of the front yard, raising a wooden cross and placing it upright in a hole.

Peterson pulled up the window, the wooden frame rattling in his hands. "Anthony?"

"Oh, hey, Dad."

"What are you doing?"

The porch light clicked on next door, and Mrs. Ellis, in a plaid flannel nightgown, came out of her house. "What's happening here?" she said. Her white hair shimmered in the darkness. "Russell?"

"Hello, Mrs. Ellis," Peterson said, leaning out the window.

"Oh, you're up there?" she said. "Well, who is this?"

"It's me, Mrs. Ellis," Anthony said.

"Anthony, honey, what are you doing there?" Mrs. Ellis said.

Genice climbed out of bed and looked over Peterson's shoulder. "Russell?" she said. "What's going on?"

"It's our teenage son."

"This piece, I think I'll call, *Irony*." Anthony said. "Or *Turning Inward*."

By the time Peterson got downstairs and out the front door, the cross stood ablaze, flames whipping off the gas-soaked two-by-fours. Music was playing. Beside the cross sat Anthony's boom box. John Coltrane's "Favorite Things" noodled and bopped out into the crisp, springtime air.

Mrs. Ellis stood on her porch, her arms crossed over her chest, watching.

Anthony sat on the sidewalk across the street snapping photos with his digital camera. "Wake up, everybody!" he said. There was not a smile on his face exactly, but it glowed with a bliss Peterson couldn't understand.

"Put it out now!" Peterson said.

"Just a minute," Anthony said, leaning over to watch the cross burn in his own front yard. He snapped a few more photos. "Turn around, Dad," he said. "Just stop for a second, and think about it."

Porch lights up and down the street snapped on and neighbors stepped out of their houses.

Genice, in a pink terry cloth bathrobe, came outside and started uncoiling the garden hose. "Anthony!" she shouted. "Do what your father says."

Anthony's little sisters, Kaneesha and Tyra, shuffled out in their pajamas. "Mom, what's going on?"

"Don't worry," she said. "It's just Anthony."

Peterson turned away from his son and moved across the lawn, kicking at the cross with his slippered feet. The flames whipped and the embers cracked and popped as the cross toppled over onto the grass. Peterson took the hose from Genice and attempted to douse the flames. He looked up, around the neighborhood, at Mrs. Ellis, and the rest of the white faces standing ghostlike under their yellowy porch lights. "It's all right, everybody. Sorry to wake you. There's no problem here. Just Anthony!"

They nodded and crept back into their darkened homes, leaving the Petersons alone with their cross and their blaring jazz music.

Peterson carried the hose to Anthony's boom box and sprayed it for several seconds. Coltrane's saxophone gurgled through the wet speakers as the sound of sirens crept closer and closer. Anthony sat across the street laughing and applauding. He stood up and walked onto the lawn.

"That was a perfect ending," he said.

"You're crazy," Kaneesha said.

Tyra shook her head. "That's right, you're messed up."

A squad car pulled up to the house, followed by a fire truck. Officer Powell and his occasional partner, the portly, retired stonemason, Claude Burrows, climbed out of the car.

"Good evening, Dr. Peterson," Officer Powell said. "How you doing tonight, Mrs. Peterson? Anthony up to his usual?"

"Just one of his stunts," Peterson said. "Everything is fine. You know how Anthony is."

Anthony walked up to the Officer Powell and offered his

hand. "Thanks for coming out, Ernie. You should've seen it. I think I got some good shots." He held up his camera. "With that," he said, moving to the front door, "I bid you all *adieu*." He snapped a photo of all of them standing there, and then turned and went inside.

Peterson looked around at his wife and daughters, at Officer Powell, Claude Burrows, and the firemen milling about their fire truck, awaiting instruction.

"Well," Officer Powell said, rubbing his blond goatee with his index finger, "what should I write in my report, Dr. Peterson?"

"Why you asking me?"

"Russell," Genice snapped.

"What?" he said. "How do I know what the hell to write? Say it's vandalism. A hate crime. A self-hate crime. Write whatever the hell you want."

"You want to press charges?" Claude Burrows said.

"What?" Peterson said, thinking for a moment. "Actually that's exactly what I want to do."

"Russell, stop it," Genice said. "We'll take care of it."

"We can take him in," Claude Burrows said, clutching the blue suspenders that stretched up either side of his enormous belly. "We could scare him straight."

Officer Powell shook his head. "Dr. Peterson, why don't you let me talk to him?"

"What?" Peterson said. "I think I can talk to my own son."

"Okay," Officer Powell said. "It's just that me and Anthony, I don't know, ever since that thing out at Holmes Road Bridge, we kind of, in a way, reached an understanding."

"Seems like he's acting out or something," Claude Burrows said.

"Oh, you think so?" Peterson said. "Is that your professional opinion?"

He turned, went into the house and took the stairs two at a time. He rushed down the hall, stopped at Anthony's door, and tried the handle. It was locked, again. "Anthony, open the door."

"I told you, I'm not doing drugs."

"Officer Powell wants me to press charges."

"For real? Can I go to jail?"

"Goddammit," Peterson said. He leaned back and kicked at the door. It boomed and rattled, but didn't open. Several months ago Anthony had installed a large dead bolt, and whenever Peterson heard it click an aggravation rose in him, and he had to take a deep breath to calm himself. He stepped back and tried ramming the door with his shoulder.

"What are you doing?" Genice shouted, as she came up the stairs. "Are you going crazy?"

"I don't know what to do, Genice," he said. "Tell me what to do." He turned and went into their bedroom, slamming the door behind him.

On his way to work the next morning, Peterson stopped at the dry cleaner's to drop off some of his shirts and a dress for Genice. Peterson walked through the door, the bell jingling above his head. Michael Phu sat behind the counter, shelling pistachios. He stood up and wiped his pink fingers on a paper towel. "Good morning, Dr. Peterson. How are you today?"

"Good, good," Peterson said. "How's that crown feeling?"

"Oh, I don't even know it's there most the time," Michael

Phu said, his thick accent and staccato inflection making it hard to understand. "Feel like real tooth."

Peterson leaned forward and tried to grasp every word. He didn't want to be one of those people who smiled and said, "Yes, very good," to everything Michael Phu said.

"I'm so glad," Peterson said.

Michael Phu took the clothes from Peterson and hung them on the metal bar beside the cash register. "I heard about Anthony last night," he said. "Everything okay?"

"What? Oh, yeah, sure. Everything's good. You know Anthony," Peterson said, with a chuckle. "Hey, I heard that Cherilyn got into Harvard."

"She hard worker. Always do her work. I wish her mother still here to see how good she is. But I tell myself, everything happen for reason."

"Yes," Peterson said. "Mrs. Phu, she was a real nice lady."

Michael nodded and cleared his throat. "So, is Anthony going to college? Some art school or something? Very creative."

"Oh, I don't know what to tell you, Michael. We're trying to talk him into going to a real college, the University of Vermont, or even New Hampshire. You know, get a good education, do something useful."

"That good." Michael Phu said. "That very good,"

Peterson drove through the small downtown, past Frigate's Ice Cream Landing, Green Mountain Bank, and the Candlery, before turning down Hogarth, to his office, a blocky, one-story clapboard structure built just after World War II by Dr. Cuthpert, who practiced his primitive dentistry until two days before his ninety-first birthday. There are legends still floating around town of wrongly-pulled teeth and the near-overdosing of many children from too much Novocaine. But Dr. Cuthpert maintained the respect of the community by donating most of the money to build what is now Cuthpert Gymnasium, where the high school basketball games are played, and to Cuthpert Auditorium, where the local theatrical events—dance and piano recitals, the community theater, and the high school plays—are performed. Peterson often wondered if he too could get his name on a building in town, The R. Peterson Community Center, or Peterson Public Library, with a little plaque by the door, commemorating the unique life of the generous benefactor, his rise from poverty to patron.

Peterson parked his car and went into the office, not surprised to see his secretary, Samantha Runyan, surfing the 'Net. "Good morning, Sam," he said. "Have you got the coffee started? I'm beat."

"Oh, my," she said, pointing at her computer screen. "Is that you?"

Peterson set his briefcase down and looked over her shoulder at the image of a black man in a bathrobe kicking over a burning cross. Red and orange flames shattered the darkness and the bathrobe shimmered blue in the foreground. Beside the photo a headline from the local paper's web site barked out *Black Boy Burns Cross in Own Yard.*

Sam scrolled down to another, smaller photo of the same man standing over a few flickering flames, a garden hose in his hand.

She looked up at his blank face. "Are you all right, Russ?"

"I don't get it," he said. "Why would he do that?"

"I've been there," she said, her eyebrows pushed up on her forehead. "With Megan I never knew what to do."

He carried his briefcase into his office, took off his jacket, and hung it on the coatrack behind the door. He slipped into his white coat and pulled his goggles over his head. Then he stopped and stared at the coat rack for a moment before grabbing and hurling it across the room. It bounced off the wall and sent two of his glass-framed diplomas crashing to the floor.

His breath came out in short bursts as he stood looking down at the fragments of glass sparkling on the beige tile.

The door opened and Samantha leaned in. "Russ? Are you okay?"

"Close the door," he said.

"I understand. Really. When Megan got pregnant, I just about thought I was going to kill her. And I tried everything with her, God knows it. But they're teenagers, you know . . ."

"I don't have any emergencies today, do I? No root canals or anything?"

"No," she said, "no one's called in with anything. Just some checkups and those fillings for Mr. Uhle. He called again this morning just to confirm. You know what a worrywart he is."

"Cancel my appointments."

"Sure," she said, coming into the room and picking up the coat rack. "With Megan, I did everything I could." She shook out the shards of glass from his jacket. "Now I don't even know where she's at. Last I talked to her, she was cleaning rooms at a Motel 6 in Portland."

On his way home Peterson drove the streets that had become, in the past year, his son's workshop, studio, and gallery. Anthony had created and displayed his work all over town. Peterson drove across Holmes Road Bridge, the place where, last summer, it all started.

Anthony had painted a large black penis above the arching trusses. Erect, it measured almost ten feet. One cloudy Sunday morning Officer Powell supervised Anthony as he painted over the penis with the industrial gray paint of the original bridge. They laughed and talked, telling jokes and stories to pass the time, and then when they parted, they exchanged email addresses, all while Peterson sat in his car reading the paper, occasionally glancing up and watching them in disbelief.

Anthony received a sentence of thirty hours of community service for the stunt. Every Saturday morning for two months Peterson dropped him off at the Boys Club down on Beacon, where he taught arts and crafts to elementary school kids. Peterson was surprised to hear that all Anthony had taught them was how to draw birds and flowers and not enormously oversized genitalia.

And then there was that Sunday last fall, when, at two-thirty in the afternoon, Anthony wandered all over town dressed as a clown in whiteface, shouting into a blowhorn. "Hey everybody! It's time to wake up!" He stood on various street corners, in front of the large colonial homes on Manley Street, urging people who were obviously not asleep to wake up. "Wake up! Hey, you in there! Wake up!"

Peterson remembered his meeting with Anthony's art teacher, Ms. Schoenberg, after Anthony was found painting a mural on the wall outside the auto shop of a black Jesus on the cross in U.S. Army Fatigues with a tube of Jheri Curl in one hand and a basketball in the other. She kept saying that Anthony was uniquely talented, as if this legitimized his outrageous behavior.

When Peterson got home, he climbed out of the car and

looked down at the lawn his son had ruined the night before. Anthony had refilled the hole and carried the charred two-by-fours over to the garbage cans beside the garage. But the black soot and burned grass remained, and until it grew out, the front lawn would bear the scar of a cross.

He entered the quiet, empty house and climbed the stairs to Anthony's room, where he stared down at the lock. He shook his head and went into his bedroom and changed into jeans and a sweatshirt and then hiked down the stairs and into the garage. The ladder lay on the floor along the wall. He picked it up somewhere in the middle, trying to balance it as best he could, and carried it out of the garage, and through the front yard, to the side of the house.

Mrs. Ellis sat up in her rose garden. "Hello, Russell, how are you today?" There was a smudge above her right eyebrow, and her bushy, white hair spilled over the top and sides of her beige visor.

"Oh, I'm fine. How are you, Mrs. Ellis?"

"Took the day off, did you?"

Peterson placed the ladder under his son's bedroom window and pressed his foot on the bottom rung to secure it.

"Isn't that Anthony's room?" Mrs. Ellis asked.

Peterson started up the ladder.

"Be careful now," she said, coming into his yard. "You want me to hold that for you?"

"No, thank you, Mrs. Ellis. I'll be all right."

She grabbed the ladder and put one foot on the bottom rung. "Here now, I've got it down here. You should be just fine. There is a bit of a breeze though. Be careful up there."

"Mrs. Ellis, there's no need, really, I'm fine." He climbed to the top of the ladder and saw that Anthony's window was not latched shut. He tried to force it open but the old wooden frame was warped and unforgiving.

Mrs. Ellis stepped back as he worked his way down the ladder.

"Can't get it open?" she said.

Peterson shook his head and went to the garage to get a crowbar. When he came back around the house, Mrs. Ellis was up the ladder, peering into Anthony's bedroom. "Mrs. Ellis," he said. "What are you doing up there?"

"It's kind of a funny room, isn't it?"

"Mrs. Ellis," he snapped, "will you please get down?"

"What is all that on the walls?" She climbed down the ladder. "He is an interesting boy, isn't he?" She stopped on the bottom rung and thought for a moment.

"Excuse me, Mrs. Ellis," Peterson said. He climbed up the ladder and pried the window open just enough to wiggle his way through.

When he stood up and looked around he was surprised to see how organized everything was. The room was immaculate. The bed was made, the books on the shelf alphabetized by the authors' last names. A mosaic of paint, tiles, magazine clippings and photographs covered all four walls. Figures of African women danced inside a giant white face stretched into a scream. A broken yellow umbrella stood upside down by a manhole cover. There were jazz musicians, bent back, their horns blaring up to the red sky above them. There were birds, flowers, a brightly-lit Ferris wheel. And in the middle of it all, a newspaper headline read: *Man in Need of Heart.*

He sat on the bed and looked up at the black ceiling. Words, in bright white, had been written up there. He leaned back on his elbows and tried to decipher them. The first word was *WAKE.*

Staring straight up from his pillow, this is what Anthony read every morning. *WAKE UP!*

Peterson rolled off the bed and began looking through Anthony's Pollock-inspired paint-splattered bureau. Clothes, neatly folded, filled the first three drawers. The bottom two were stuffed with hundreds of photos—black-and-white, color and sepia-toned photos of leaves floating on a dark pond; oddly shaped shadows and sunlight on dark pavement; dead, rotting trees with flowers blooming out of the moss; a shoe tilted on its side on a dry, cracked sidewalk.

Peterson turned and opened the closet. Inside was a small darkroom. Pans of solution sat on a narrow table, and above them several photos hung on a line to dry. He leaned into the closet and glanced at the photos, grabbing one and pulling it off the line to look at it in the light of the room. It was a grainy, color photo of Cherilyn Phu, Michael Phu's Harvard-bound daughter, standing naked in front of a mound of blue glass, her hair spiked up all over her head and her arms hanging down at her sides. Her red fingernails, which matched her red platform shoes, lightly touched her pale thighs. She faced the camera straight on, her legs spread apart, her pubic hair wisping up, and her defiant, upturned breasts laying claim to some mysterious person she was just now becoming.

He went into the closet and grabbed more photos—Cherilyn Phu lying naked, her body submerged in a heap of green beer bottles; Cherilyn sitting on a plastic yellow chair in front of a mountain of brown glass; her naked body rising out of an old washing machine, her arms thrusting into the sky with a sheepish grin on her face; Cherilyn peeking out from behind a rusty dryer, her black hair now falling over her eyes. In this place of used-up things, of rust and decomposition, she was utterly new. She was unspeakably beautiful, or the photos were, or both. Peterson couldn't tell which.

He pulled the cell phone from his pocket and called Genice at her office at the school administration building. She said she was too busy to talk. "A woman from the State Board of Ed. decided to drop in on us this morning. An informal inspection or something."

Peterson asked if she could meet him for lunch at El Burro, the new Mexican restaurant out on the highway.

"Is everything okay?" she asked.

When she came into the restaurant, Peterson was in the bar in jeans and a sweatshirt, sipping a strawberry margarita. "What's going on?" she said, pointing at his drink.

"Oh," he said. "I had Sam cancel my appointments today."

"Why?"

"Come on," he said. "Let's get something to eat."

They went into the dining room and sat at a table by the window that overlooked the parking lot. A young waitress came over with a couple of menus, a basket of chips, and a bowl of salsa. She stopped and stared at Peterson before turning around and heading back to the kitchen.

"What was that about?" Genice said.

"I have no idea." Peterson picked up a chip and started eating.

"Russell," Genice said. "What's going on? I really shouldn't be away from the office right now."

"How'd the inspection go?"

"I don't know. It's not over yet. She's still there checking our files."

"Genice," he said, leaning over the table. "I made a mistake. A big mistake."

"What are you talking about?"

"I've been thinking a lot lately, about a lot of things," he said, his voice hushed and unsteady. "About my father."

"Oh, your father again."

"Genice." He shook his head, dipping a chip into the salsa. "A waste of time, that's what he said, remember? A waste of time. No matter how much education you get, it won't matter. They'll only let you climb so high."

"I know, I know."

"So what do I do? I mean, I have to prove him wrong, right? So I move you and the kids out here, where I can make a lot of money, and we can live in a huge house in some Norman Rockwell painting, and hey, look at us, we've got everything we ever wanted. And in the process, of course, our son goes insane."

"You're not serious," she said.

"Genice, there are pictures of me on the Internet in my bathrobe, kicking that fucking cross. The entire world can see what he's doing. And everybody around here knows. They all know."

"So, what are you proposing?"

"I think we should seriously consider moving back to Boston."

Genice looked down at the table, her jaw clenched. "So," she said, "let me get this straight. We moved out here because you have issues with your father, and now you want to uproot us, again, because you can't stand your own son?"

"What?"

"I was against moving out here. Remember? I fought you on

it. But you just had to do it. And so I shut my mouth and did what I was supposed to do. And you know what? I'm happy I did it. It's taken a long time to make this work, a long time. But now we have friends here, Russell, and the kids are in good schools, and the neighborhoods are safe."

"Yeah, but what about Anthony?"

"Russell, first of all, I'm not moving. You need to get that in your head right now. And second, you need to open your ears and listen to the boy, really listen to what he's saying, and when he pulls one of his stunts, then we should be firm without disrespecting him. Right now you just yell at him. That's all you do."

"Genice, I went into his room this morning."

"What?"

"Have you been in there? I thought I might find drugs or something."

"Russell, he's not doing drugs."

"I think there's something seriously wrong with him. He painted his walls, and his ceiling is black."

"I've been in his room. He lets me in, probably because I don't scream at him all the time."

"I found some photos he took."

"Yeah? Of what?"

"I don't know," he said. "Just photos, you know, of different things."

That night they sat down to dinner, and Genice told Anthony that she and Peterson had decided to ground him for a week for burning the cross. Anthony took it in and continued eating.

"That means no TV," Genice said. "No phone. No Internet. You're just to go to your room, do homework, or read a book or something. Got it?"

Anthony nodded and wiped his mouth.

Peterson watched his son as Kaneesha told a story about a new boy in class who wore overalls and how the kids all started calling him Farmer.

Tyra laughed. "Farmer," she said.

Anthony finished eating, and as he got up to go to his room, he turned back and said, "I'm sorry for getting you guys involved." He nodded and then left the room.

Peterson looked at Genice, amazed. "Did he just say what I thought he said?"

"People at school think he's crazy," Tyra said.

After dinner Peterson sat down in the living room to watch TV. He pressed his thumb on the remote, stopping on the lotto drawing to watch as the white balls tumbled out. "17! 42! 23!"

"Thank you, everybody!" Anthony shouted, shuffling down the stairs, a backpack slung over his shoulder. "Mom, I'm outta here! I don't know when I'll be back!"

Genice came out of the kitchen. "What did you say?"

"I'm escaping this prison. Someone went into my room today," he said, staring at Peterson. "Someone was in my room without asking me first." He clenched his jaw and inhaled through his nose. "I'm feeling a little violated right now."

"What?" Peterson said, rising to his feet. "Is this some joke? *You* feel violated? I'm on the Internet in my bathrobe! How do you think *I* feel? My son burns a cross in my front yard, and he feels violated. That's just great."

"Russell," Genice said. She turned to Anthony. "Honey, just have a seat. We can talk this out."

"You don't just go into my room," Anthony said, his voice cracking.

"Well, last I checked, this is my house. I can go into any room I want."

"Yes, massuh," Anthony said. "Yessuh, massuh."

"Anthony," Genice said.

"No," Anthony said. "You're not the master. You're a slave." He thrust his fist into the air. "Live free or die."

"Jesus," Peterson said. "Are you listening to this, Genice?"

"Are *you* listening to it?" she said.

"It's like my voice is silent to you, Dad," Anthony said, opening the front door. "It's gibberish, it's music to your tone-deaf ears. Mom, I'll be at David's." He walked out, slamming the door behind him.

Genice wiped her hands on a dishcloth and cleared her throat, staring at the door. She turned and looked up at Kaneesha and Tyra, who stood at the top of the stairs in their leotards and ballet slippers. "Okay," she said. "Show's over, girls. You can go back to your room now."

"Yep," Peterson said, forcing a smile. "Recital's tomorrow night. You better get practicing. Don't you want it to be special?"

The girls looked at each other, and then down at Genice.

"Go on," she said. "Get back to your practice. I want to hear some music up there."

When the girls disappeared Genice looked back at Peterson and shook her head. Then she went back into the kitchen, fumbled with some dishes, and slammed a cupboard door.

"Six American soldiers killed in Iraq," a newscaster's voice barked from the TV. "More at eleven."

After another sleepless night Peterson's chest and stomach felt hollowed out. A mild, hazy ache filled his head, blurring his peripheral vision. He climbed into his car and drove the streets of Severston, looking for his son, circling the neighborhoods between David's house and the high school, past the saggy-panted teenage boys shoving one another on the sidewalks and the long-haired smokers standing back from the road under the blossoming trees.

As he turned onto Langston Street, he noticed Cherilyn Phu, walking by herself. She was wearing a short, plaid skirt that hung to mid-thigh, with red socks pulled up to her knees, and in her hands she carried a small loaf of bread.

He pulled over and rolled down the passenger side window. "Good morning, Cherilyn."

"Oh, hey, Dr. Peterson."

She smiled at him, the upturned corners of her mouth sending him back to Anthony's room and the photo of her standing naked in a washing machine, her hands above her head, with that same smile on her face.

"Listen," he said, noticing that her thick black hair was swept to the side and held down by a butterfly barrette. "Have you seen Anthony?"

"No," she said. "I'm sorry, I haven't."

"Well, if you do, could you tell him I'm looking for him?"

"Sure. Is everything okay?"

"Oh, yeah. He just forgot his homework."

"You want me to bring it to him?"

"Huh? Oh, no," he said. "That's all right. I'll just drop it off at school."

"All right. Have a good day."

"You too."

He watched her as she walked down the sidewalk, shocked that such a normal-looking girl, almost homely, could be so stunning on film. He imagined her in the recycling yard bending over, taking off her clothes, and then standing up, naked, with the confidence and beauty she had never possessed before. How did Anthony know, and how did he bring that quality out in her?

Peterson put the car in gear and pulled up beside her again. "Hey, Cherilyn," he said.

"Why don't you hop in? I'll give you a lift."

"Oh, well, thanks, but it's only a couple more blocks," she said.

"It's no problem. I'm going there anyway."

She shrugged and got into the car, placing the loaf of bread on her lap.

"Well," Peterson said, smiling at her. "What's that you have there?"

"This? Oh, it's just a pistachio-nut bread my father made for Mrs. Thompson. She wrote a recommendation letter for me."

"Well, that's nice." He pressed on the gas and said, "Congratulations on getting into Harvard. That's quite an accomplishment."

"Oh, I got lucky."

"I don't think that's true."

Peterson drove down Langston, and then at the four-way stop, he got behind a school bus turning onto Northbrook. There was a line of cars and buses heading into the parking lot, but Peterson veered right and drove past the school, his heart jumping in his chest.

"Um, Dr. Peterson?" Cherilyn said. "That was the school."

"It was?" he said.

"We just passed it."

"Oh. Well, Cherilyn, I need to go someplace first."

"But I can't miss my first class."

"Don't worry about it," he said, trying to calm her. "I'll get you there in a few minutes. I promise." He wondered if Anthony had used the antique folding camera he and Genice had given him as a Christmas present. Was that why there was a slight blurring around the edge of photos?

He turned onto Old Mill Road and pushed on the gas, sending them out past Trump's Orchard and Lake Simmons. Sunlight shimmered on the moist leaves of the apple and dogwood trees.

"Where are we going?" Cherilyn said. "Dr. Peterson?"

"Cherilyn, I promise you'll be back at school in a few minutes."

He pulled off at the landfill, and turned onto an unnamed dirt road that wound down to the recycling center. He brought the car to a stop beside a row of dumpsters and a chain-link fence lined with trash. He shut off the car and looked through the windshield at the stack of newspapers that ran along the other side of the fence.

"What are we doing here?" Cherilyn asked.

"I just need to see something," he said. He opened the door and got out of the car. "C'mon," he said, trying to sound as casual as possible.

He pushed through the gate and walked into the recycling yard, where aluminum cans, and glass and plastic bottles were soon to be transformed into park benches and teeter-totters. On this outside slab of concrete, everything had been separated into different mounds that would be scooped up and carried into the building at the far end. Nobody was here. It was quiet, and the rotten smell from the nearby landfill hung in the air.

Peterson heard the car door open and close, and then the slow shuffling of Cherilyn's feet as she walked into the yard and stopped just inside the gate.

He turned and walked up to a large pile of blue bottles, some still whole, others in shards. He stared at it for a moment, imagining her climbing onto the pile and lying down, her alabaster skin on the blue glass.

"Oh, my God," Cherilyn said, under her breath, but loud enough for Peterson to hear.

"Yeah," he said, giving a small nod.

"He told me nobody would see them," she said. "He promised."

"I went into his room," he said, looking down at the gray, cracked concrete, and shaking his head. "I'm sorry. I found them."

"Dr. Peterson, I'm sorry."

"Can I ask you something?" he said.

"Look, I really need to get back to school."

"Why did you do it?"

"I've got a midterm in Global."

"Cherilyn, why did you let him take pictures of you out here?"

She looked around, searching for an answer.

"Did he offer you money?"

"No."

Peterson clasped his hands in front of his face and shook them back and forth. "So, let me get this straight, okay? Some kid asks you to take off your clothes out here, in public, with all this trash, and you say, *Sure, no problem, where do you want me to stand?*"

"Dr. Peterson, I don't think you get it."

"No, obviously I don't."

"There's just something about him," she said. "He's not like anybody else. I mean, he's an artist."

"Come on, Cherilyn, you're going to Harvard, for God's sake." Peterson ran his hand over his forehead, then turned away from her and walked over to the washing machine and looked inside at its rusty barrel.

"This is just trash," he said. "A bunch of garbage."

He turned to the mound of blue glass, stopping at the sight of himself, the dark outline of his reflection in various shapes and sizes, in front of a bright, azure sky. "You were right here," he said.

"Dr. Peterson, I really need to get back to school."

"You looked like you were floating. Like you were in some strange . . ." He couldn't complete his thought. What was she floating in? He turned and walked toward her. "Cherilyn, come here."

"Dr. Peterson, please," she said, stepping back. "No."

He grabbed her right arm and pulled her to the mound of blue glass.

"Dr. Peterson," she said, struggling against him.

"Please," he said, "just . . . Cherilyn, just stand right here. Okay?" He backed up, trying to picture her inside the frame of a camera lens.

She stood there, her arms folded in front of her, looking away, tears filling her eyes. Here was the homely girl he always knew. Nothing special. An average girl in front of a mound of glass. He pictured his son's photos and thought of him out here, right in this position with a camera in his hand, capturing a strikingly different Cherilyn.

"Have you seen them?" he said to her. "The photos? Do you have any idea what you look like?"

She took a deep breath and shook her head, and then reached up and wiped her tears with the back of her hand.

Peterson drove quickly, silently, keeping his eyes on the road, away from Cherilyn, who sat beside him, equally quiet.

"That bread sure smells good," he said.

Cherilyn didn't respond.

"I didn't know your father liked to bake," he said. He turned from Old Mill Road onto Northbrook, with the school visible just down the block. "I guess there's a lot about your father I don't know."

He turned into the empty parking lot in front of the school. "Here we are," he said.

As he brought the car to a stop, he heard sniffling, and finally turned to look at her.

"Now I'm late," she said. She held her hand over her eyes, and with her index finger and thumb she pressed the bridge of her nose. "My dad's going to kill me."

"Listen, Cherilyn," he said. "I really am sorry."

"Yeah?" she said, and then turned to him. "Go fuck yourself." She opened the door and climbed out of the car. "I'm going to tell everyone about this," she said. "You're fucking crazy!" She slammed the door and, with the loaf of bread in her hands and the backpack slung over her shoulder, she ran up the steps, under the giant blue and white mural that read, "Falcons Soar to Victory." She pulled open the door and disappeared inside the school.

Peterson sat there, stunned, her words repeating themselves in his head. What did she mean, "tell everyone"? And what exactly would she say? Would she exaggerate, or make something up? He put the car in gear and pulled out of the parking lot. As he turned onto Northbrook, he imagined trying to explain himself to Genice, his children, his patients. How would the community react to him abducting a teenage girl? Would there be a write-up in the *Post Gazette*? What would the headline say? Would there be more pictures of him on the 'Net? He jerked on the wheel and turned immediately back into the parking lot. He jammed on the brakes and jumped out, leaving the car in the fire zone, and rushed up the steps, through the same doors Cherilyn had gone through just moments before.

He turned into the principal's office and walked under the flood of fluorescent lights up to the front desk. Two students sat in orange chairs, looking put out, guilty of something they'd swear they didn't do. Diane Hurtz, one of Genice's good friends, and the principal's secretary, sat behind her white computer monitor, eating a breakfast sandwich.

"Diane?"

"Oh," she said, leaning over and setting her sandwich down on its crinkled, yellow wrapper. "Dr. Peterson, how are you?"

"Can you tell me where Mrs. Thompson's room is?"

"Is everything okay? Did Anthony do something?"

"No," he said. "Everything's fine. I just have some homework he left behind. No big deal."

"Oh, well, you'll find Mrs. Thompson on the other side of the school, in the Red Wing. You know where the cafeteria is? Well you go around that, or you can go right through it too, and then . . ."

"Just a room number," Peterson interrupted. "That's all I need."

"Are you sure you're okay? You look a little flustered."

"No, no," he said. "I'm right as rain."

"Oh, okay." She pursed her lips and looked down at a sheet of light blue paper. "She's in room 29."

Peterson rushed out of the office and jogged down the hallway, past classrooms with green doors hanging open. Mr. Anderson's voice echoed out into the hallway. "Convex, from the Latin, *convehere*, is a curving outward, an arch." A student in another classroom shouted, "Why can't we all go to the library together?" Just past the dark wood trophy case and a large, pink banner hanging from the ceiling that said, *Spring Fling*, he turned into the cafeteria where Abel Trugard, the old janitor, was swirling a mop around the already shiny floor. "Hey, Dr. Peterson."

"Morning, Mr. Trugard. How are those dentures?"

"Biting and smiling."

"Good to hear."

Peterson rushed through the cafeteria and turned right, past the janitor's office and the art class. He knocked on Mrs. Thompson's bright red door, and then opened it and leaned in. The entire class, bent over their desks, silently working on a test, turned to look at him. Cherilyn, sitting in the second seat in the center aisle, peered up at him in disbelief, then shook her head and went immediately back to the exam. Anthony, in the back corner of the room, looked at his buddy next to him, leaned back and shook his head. "No," he said. "No way."

Mrs. Thompson set her book down on her desk and went to the door. "Good morning, Dr. Peterson," she whispered. "What can I help you with?"

He tried to catch his breath.

"Is everything all right?" Mrs. Thompson said. "Do you need to speak to Anthony?"

"No," he said. "I mean, yes, everything's okay. But no, I don't need to speak to Anthony. If I could, Mrs. Thompson, just have a second with Miss Phu? Just a brief moment."

"Well, she's taking a test, and she was late this morning. I don't think she has much time to finish. Can it wait for after class?"

"It's real important," he said. "It won't take more than a minute."

Mrs. Thompson forced a smile at him. "All right," she said. She went to Cherilyn and whispered in her ear.

"What?" Cherilyn said. "Nope, sorry."

"What's going on?" Anthony said. "Dad?"

"Anthony," Mrs. Thompson said. "Just concentrate on your work, please."

Peterson stood in the doorway, while Mrs. Thompson whispered to Cherilyn. He heard her say, "I'll give you more time later, Cherilyn, but right now Dr. Peterson needs to speak with you."

Cherilyn got out of her seat and walked to the door.

"Dad?" Anthony said. "What are you doing?"

Mrs. Thompson raised her hand. "Please remain quiet, Anthony!"

"Thanks a lot," Peterson said, nodding and smiling at Mrs. Thompson. "It'll just be a minute."

Cherilyn moved past him into the hallway, and he closed the

door. When he turned around her arms were crossed. She looked away from him, her lips folded up under her incisors.

"Cherilyn," he said. "Look, I'm sorry."

Just then Abel Trugard appeared down the hallway, sloshing his mop over the floor. Peterson leaned in and lowered his voice. "I shouldn't have done that, but . . ."

"You're fucking crazy," Cherilyn said, loud enough for Abel to hear. "And everybody's going to know about it. Everybody. Know what I'm saying?" She tried to move past him.

He stepped in front of her and said, "Those pictures, Cherilyn, it would be a real shame if they got on the Internet."

She stopped and stared up at him.

"If the people at Harvard saw them, or your father. How would he like those pictures?" He leaned toward her, breathing heavier than he wanted to. "My guess is he wouldn't like them at all. My guess is your father doesn't give a damn about whether or not my son is an artist."

"Is everything all right?" Abel said, his voice echoing down the hall.

"Everything's fine, Mr. Trugard," Peterson said, giving a reassuring nod.

He turned back to Cherilyn. "Nothing happened this morning, okay?" he whispered. "No pictures were taken. I'm not even here talking to you about this. We're talking about what your father might like as a gift. How about that? For all the hard work he does. Just a little token of my gratitude."

She thought about it for a moment, her eyes scanning the floor between their feet.

"So," he said, "what do you think your father would like, just as kind of an appreciation gift?"

"I don't know," she said, defeated. "I have no idea." She walked around him and opened the door.

"Good luck on the test," he said. He leaned into the room and said, "Thanks, Mrs. Thompson. I appreciate it."

"Mrs. T?" Anthony said, rising from his seat. "Can I talk to him for a minute?"

"Anthony," she said, "sit down and finish the test."

Peterson closed the door and walked through the school, with its color-coded hallways, back to his car, which sat, idling, in the fire zone, with the driver side door hanging open.

He drove across town to his office, where he had enough appointments to stay busy throughout the day. Sam brought in cups of coffee at fifteen-minute intervals to keep him alert over the open mouths of Hollis Burton and Caroline Fetterly. And then that afternoon, Claude Burrows came in with a fractured molar. "There was a rock in my chowder," he said. "If I was a Californian I'd probably sue that damn company. You know how they are out there. They'd sue you just for lookin' at 'em crooked."

Peterson gave him four injections, and as the Novocaine began to take affect, Claude started rambling. "Doc," he said, reclined in the chair, his surprisingly long, smooth fingers clasped on his enormous belly. "They have these boot camps now, you know, for wayward teens and such. Have you thought about that? I mean, I don't think Ernie, with this social work thing, I don't know, you tell me, does talking ever really work? I mean, he's a police officer not a social worker. These kids, they need discipline. Teenagers are bad enough, but you take what Anthony is and you put him in the middle of what he's not and you're asking for trouble. Don't you think? I mean, don't get me wrong, I have nothing against you, or any of you people, for that matter, I mean, you're my dentist for God's sake, and how's that wife of yours? Very pretty lady."

"Open wide," Peterson said.

Later that afternoon, after Claude stumbled out to his car with a handkerchief held to his slack lips, Peterson sat at his desk, exhausted. His head pounded, and his hands shook from all the coffee.

He put on his jacket, said good bye to Sam and left a little early, driving down Brotton Street, past Hurley's Gas 'N' Go and Sylvia's Shoe Shop, before pulling into the parking lot at Phu's Dry Cleaners. He got out of the car and stopped at the front door, thinking of what he had done that morning, and then turned around and got back into the car. He could tell Genice that her dress wasn't ready. But she would call, and Michael Phu would expose the lie. He could tell her he forgot to pick it up. He closed his eyes and sat for a moment with his head lolled back on the headrest. Genice's voice rang out in his mind, *"What do you mean, you forgot? This is a big night for the girls, and I wanted to wear that dress."*

He pulled on the door handle and climbed out of the car. Peterson had learned long ago that when choosing sides in any conflict it was wisest to agree with his wife, not only because she was usually right, but also because when he didn't, the price he paid was higher than the alternative.

The small bell rang overhead as he pushed through the front door of Phu's Cleaners. The store was empty. Machines in the back room buzzed and clattered. The sour smell of solvents hung in the air. "Hello?" Peterson called out. "Michael?"

He waited for a moment and then Cherilyn came out of the back room. She stopped, surprised, and stared at him.

"Hi, Cherilyn."

She crossed her arms, standing back away from the counter, silent. She had changed from the skirt she wore that morning into a pair of tight blue jeans.

"I just came to pick up some clothes."

"You got a ticket?"

"Oh, yeah." He searched his pockets. "It's in here somewhere."

"Just set it on the counter," she said.

"Cherilyn." He smiled at her, setting the ticket beside the register.

She grabbed the ticket and stepped back.

"Cherilyn, just listen to me, okay?"

She turned away from him, and walked into the back room.

"Cherilyn!"

The bell clanged, and Michael Phu came into the store, a bag of groceries in his hand. "Hello, Dr. Peterson. How are you today?"

"Doing fine. Just fine. How are you, Michael?"

"Not as good as some, better than others."

Peterson chuckled, even though he didn't completely understand what Michael had said. Michael came around the counter and set the bag down. "Your laundry should be ready,"

Peterson took a moment to try to grasp the words through Michael's strong, percussive accent. "Oh, yes, yes," he said. "Cherilyn is getting it for me."

"Good, good."

Peterson studied Michael. "You sure have a nice girl there, Mr. Phu. She's very impressive."

"Thank you. Hard worker. Always do her best. But today she was very bad. Late to school."

"Really?"

"She told me you pick her up." Michael said.

"What? She told you that?"

"Thank you so much. If not for you, she would have been much more late."

Cherilyn came out of the back room with Peterson's shirts and Genice's dress.

"Well, I just wanted to get her there on time," Peterson said. "I was a little surprised to see her, actually."

"You are so kind take her to school," Michael said. "So kind."

"Yeah," she said. "I don't know what I was thinking this morning. But you were right to ground me, Daddy. No TV or phone, nothing for the next two weeks. I deserve it. It was all my fault." Cherilyn glanced up at Peterson. "Well, there you go," she said, hanging the clothes on the bar beside the counter. She started ringing him up, her fingers stabbing at the keys on the register.

"Oh, I already paid," Peterson said.

Cherilyn looked up at him. "Excuse me?"

"Yes," Michael said. "Dr. Peterson always prepays."

"Oh, Daddy, Dr. Peterson told me he's going to get you a gift."

"What?" Michael said.

"What are you going to get him, Dr. Peterson?" Cherilyn said, smiling up at him.

Peterson stared at her for a moment, unable to respond.

"No gift for me," Michael said. "Please."

"No, Michael, no," Peterson stammered. "Cherilyn's right. She's absolutely right. We talked about it today, didn't we, Cherilyn, about all the great work you do for my family. I mean, our clothes are like brand new when they come out of here."

"So," Cherilyn said, "we talked about a lot of things, didn't we, Dr. Peterson? But what would you like most, Dad, a juicer, or a hamburger fryer? You're always talking about those appliances they advertise on TV. Or how about a subscription to a magazine? *Popular Mechanics?* Or a travel magazine with pictures of exotic places. You like looking at beautiful pictures."

"Nothing," Michael said. "I'm fine with what I am."

"You like *Popular Mechanics?*" Peterson said. "That's what it will be. How about that?"

"Please," Michael said.

"No, it's my pleasure, Michael, really. I'll go home right now and get a subscription for you."

"Really, Dr. Peterson . . ."

"No, I insist," Peterson said, taking his clothes. "Well, thanks. Thanks again." He looked from Michael to Cherilyn. "These are for a dance recital tonight," he said. "Down at Cuthpert Auditorium. You know, my daughters and their ballet. It's kind of a big thing for them, the spring recital."

Peterson walked out, the bell dinging over his head, and climbed into his car. He placed the clothes on the seat beside him, pulled out of the parking lot, and stopped at the one light in town. The intersection was empty. There were no cars anywhere.

The light changed from red to green and Peterson pressed on the accelerator. The sun glared down on the quiet streets, the storefronts and street signs, the telephone poles, the buttonwoods and elms that lined the road.

As he turned onto Hope Street he saw a teenage boy, a dark-skinned teenage boy, with ripped and shredded rags hanging off his body, shinnying up a mulberry tree. Peterson pulled the car off the road and sat for a minute, thinking of what to do. He punched the dashboard, and then sat back and took in a deep breath, and then let it out.

His son continued up the tree, acting as if Peterson weren't there.

Peterson rolled down the window and yelled, "Anthony! Hey!"

Anthony ignored him, working his way out onto a limb that hung over the road.

Peterson pulled on the door handle and climbed out of the car. "What are you doing up there?"

"I'm not talking to you," Anthony said, taking a thick piece of rope off his shoulder.

Peterson crossed the road. "You look like Chicken George."

"That's the point." Anthony bent down and began tying one end of the rope around the tree limb.

"Anthony, why do you have to do this?"

"I don't know," Anthony said. "Why is the sky blue?"

"You know, these stunts of yours put us in the newspaper, your mom and me. Do you think we like being in the paper? Everyone talking about us?"

"Oh, listen to this," Anthony said. "This from the dude who kidnaps my girlfriend and then fucking blackmails her."

"What?"

"You heard me. She told me all about it. You're fucking crazy."

"Enough with that word."

"What? 'Fuck'?" Anthony said. "Or 'crazy'?"

"Anthony."

"I'm not talking to you."

"So, now she's your girlfriend?" Peterson said. "Since when?"

"Since whenever I want."

"Anthony, just stop this. Okay?"

Anthony ignored him. He tugged on the rope to make sure it was secure, and then wavered and caught himself on a branch.

"You're not going to hurt yourself up there, are you?" Peterson said.

"I might," Anthony scoffed. "I've got a full-body harness under my costume. It'll only look like I'm dead."

"What if the limb breaks?"

"That's probably what you want, isn't it?"

"Why do you have to say that?"

"Cuz it's true." Anthony started wrapping the end of the rope into a noose. "So why'd you do it?" he said.

"Do what?"

"Kidnap my girlfriend."

"I didn't kidnap anybody."

"You totally freaked her out!" Anthony shouted. "And now she's talking about breaking up with me."

"Anthony, look," Peterson said. "I'm sorry about that. Okay? I'm sorry."

"Yeah, well."

"I just don't get it," Peterson said. "I don't get it."

"Everybody's always trying to get it." Anthony fixed the noose over his head and around a metal hook wrapped in cloth at the back of his neck. "Maybe you're not supposed to."

"So, this is art, huh?" Peterson said. "To you this is some artistic statement you're trying to make?"

"It is what it is."

"What's with the slave stuff? Why can't you just stick to painting? Or you could perform in a play or something, or hell, you could even rap."

"Well, let's see, why does a middle-aged dentist take a teenage girl to a recycling center at seven in the morning with nothing to recycle?"

Peterson put his hands in his pockets and looked down at the dark pavement where sunlight and shadows moved around at his feet.

Anthony sat down on the limb and started positioning himself, scooting a little to the left. "Everyone's asleep," he said. "I mean, this town, they're like snoring twenty-four seven. I mean, there's a war, right? People are dying, by the thousands, and what do these people do? They go shopping!"

"Okay."

"Art's supposed to wake you up. I mean, yeah, it can be beautiful, you know, like a picture or a statue, and it's there just to be like a reminder that beauty exists and we have a reason to be here. Okay, that's fine, but some of it should shake things up too, because the world can be a fucked-up place. It's not all gingerbread and tea, all manicures and SUV's and happy little TV commercials. Know what I'm sayin'?"

"Yeah," Peterson said. "Shit happens."

"That's a cliché," Anthony said. "But it's true."

"Well," Peterson said, "what do you want me to do? You want me to take a picture or something, call the police?"

"No," Anthony said, flashing a small black device in the palm of his hand. "I've got a remote for my two digital cameras that I've prepped for the event."

Peterson looked around, spotting one camera on a tripod behind a tree, and the other camera on a tripod tucked back in the woods on the other side of the road.

"In a little while," Anthony said, "people will be getting off work, moms driving their kids to soccer practice, asleep at the wheel, and they'll have to drive by me, a black man lynched on Hope Street. That's what I'm calling this piece: *Black Man Lynched on Hope Street.* This'll wake them up."

"Well, there's no doubt about that," Peterson said, turning away.

"That's it?" Anthony said.

"What more do you want?"

"I was just expecting something else."

"Don't we all?" Peterson said. As he crossed the street, Anthony began to lower himself from the tree limb.

"Oh," Peterson said, "Don't forget your sisters' dance recital tonight."

"I wouldn't miss that," Anthony said, before letting his body go limp, hanging from the tree ten feet above the ground, his head dangling, his eyes closed.

Peterson stopped on the edge of the road and stared up at the boy in disbelief. It was ridiculous, Anthony hanging from a tree on a spring day in Vermont. But Peterson didn't laugh, because although it wasn't pleasant, or even remotely beautiful, maybe this *was* art, maybe there was something important the boy was trying to express. This did in fact happen. People did die. Thousands of people were hanged from trees all over America, and his son was here to remind him of this, to force everyone in their small, quiet town to think about it for a moment.

Anthony opened his eyes and looked down at Peterson. "Are you going to go, or what?"

"Yeah," Peterson said, startled. "Yeah, I'm outta here."

He climbed into his car, turned the key in the ignition and pulled onto the street. After thinking about it for a moment, he turned down Manley, and drove through the historic district, past the colonial houses with their long sloping lawns, their white pillars and beveled doors. He turned back onto Brotton, and drove past the gift shops and Phu's Cleaners, where Michael Phu was out front sweeping the parking lot with a cigarette in his mouth. Peterson pressed on the horn and held up his hand as he passed through the light. And then he turned back onto Hope Street. Sunlight flashed through the trees, and shadows made random patterns on the road in front of him.

As Peterson passed under his hanging son, he turned and looked directly into the roadside camera, hoping Anthony had pressed the remote. Later, maybe in a day or two, he would ask the boy if he could see the photos, see if he'd made it to film, if he himself had become a subject in one of his son's works of art. He honked the horn, and as he continued down Hope Street, past the old mansions, through the tunnel of maple and dogwood trees, he glanced in his rearview mirror, and saw, growing smaller and smaller, the silhouette of a body hanging in the early evening sun.

Male of the Species

Threats were coming in every form—dirty looks and whispers in the grocery store, voices on the answering machine, notes under windshield wipers. *Burn in hell!* was scribbled in purple chalk on our front step. There was a brick on the bathroom floor, shards of glass from the broken window and a sheet of pink stationery creased under a rubber band, and on the paper, in looping cursive, it said: *Revelations 20:3!*

Obsessions are everywhere. In Indiana, basketball hoops rise from the ground like weeds. In Brazil, ragged soccer balls wobble through every dusty field. In Saskatchewan, children curl up at night, clutching their favorite hockey sticks. And here, in the small towns of West Texas, we're no different, we have our own obsession—one my naive Yankee husband thought was smaller than dignity, one he thought could be quelled by reason. Here, at the beginning of every school year, when the heat of the summer tapers off and the leaves begin to burn, we lose ourselves in the bleachers every Friday night. We chant in reverie and raise our hands to the Lord above, virtually speaking in tongues as the teams take the field. This is the church of the end-around, the hitch-and-go, the flea-flicker. A fumble is a sin, a missed tackle unforgivable. *Thou shalt not clip. Thou shalt not covet thy opponent's facemask. Thou shalt not use thy coach's name in vain.*

My husband, a decent man from Baraboo, Wisconsin, doesn't understand the rabid leanings of the desperate and the lonely. Where he is from cows sway in the fog, and rivers are brown, sluggish things. Fathers and mothers take their children to churches with cold pews and flaskless preachers who rarely look up from the pulpit and, if they can't be heard, aren't asked to speak up.

Since moving down here after college, he has been an outcast, "sticking out like a diamond in a goat's ass," my father commented. But my husband doesn't seem to mind. He has always been a loner, a man with no need to socialize. He is happiest sitting on the banks of the Concho, with Bradley, our sixteen-year-old, yanking a jig through the current, pointing out the grayheaded Junco, revealing the hidden spots in catalpa blossoms. He gets his fill by showing the smooth-brained adolescents at Ambrose High the inner clicking of nature—the way crawfish droppings influence the weather, how an early frost in West Texas affects the mating habits of the lemur in Madagascar.

"Science, ladies and gentleman," he starts every year, "is not about proving, or even theorizing. Science is the overturning of mushy debris, the digging up and the paring down, the uncovering of mystery, only to welcome the mysterious again and again. Science is an unending epic poem, full of adventure and enigma."

The students who didn't think he was crazy actually bought his particular brand of preaching. And the parents didn't seem to mind, as he told the kids that science and religion are not incompatible. For fifteen years he'd built an impressive career for himself, decorating his tiny office with certificates and awards. But how quickly the community turned on him, sending death threats in greeting cards, wishing him many happy years in hell.

My husband, the enemy of the people here in Ambrose, had the misfortune of seeing Jimmy Carter, the football star we call *El Presidente*, walk into his freshman biology class on the first day of school. What a senior was doing in freshman biology was beyond him, so he tried several times to transfer Jimmy into a more advanced class. The principal, Graham Phillips, my husband's only close friend here, soft-pedaled the issue until early one October day when he said, "Matthew, the boy's already rushed for fourteen hundred yards. His picture's gonna be in *Sports Illustrated*, for God's sake. Let the kid be."

Halfway through the season when Jimmy looked at the red F on his mid-term, he smiled at my husband, and as he walked out of class he was joshing with his classmates like nothing had happened. Fifteen minutes later Coach Stubbe interrupted Matthew's chemistry lecture.

"I'm in the middle of something here, Coach," my husband said. "Can it wait?" In West Texas, you don't do this to the football coach. Maybe other places, but not West Texas.

Word spread like a bad virus, and Jimmy Carter, the prize of the Permian Basin, the jovial kid who never turned in work but still somehow always got Cs, was in danger of getting yanked off the team. All because some Yankee teacher dug some moral fiber out of the black cavern of his Yankee heart. How convenient that his son just happened to be the backup.

The season rambled on, with Jimmy still on the team. Wins piled on top of wins, and as the shiny-toothed wonder boy broke tackle after tackle, he became the messiah of West Texas. ESPN showed up to "catch a glimpse of this rising star." That night Jimmy danced around and pounded through Abilene Cooper for 367 yards.

As it got closer to playoff time and as the boys moved up the 5A rankings, the academic quarter was drawing to a close and final exams were handed out.

At the end of the day Matthew flipped through the tests looking for Jimmy's. Maybe the boy had studied. Kids sometimes surprise us. Or maybe he cheated and didn't get caught. That would be okay, too. But Matthew knew without having to read the name that the sketch of a clown pointing a bulbous finger at him, the clown with a flick of a line moving from his mouth to the caption that read "Pull my finger," was Jimmy's.

The people of Ambrose couldn't say anything out loud. The pretense of righteousness is beaten into a child early on in these parts, and it just wouldn't do for people to be saying what's really on their minds, not in public anyhow. And on top of that, they didn't want it to catch wind over to Odessa, San Angelo, or Abilene, where our opponents' media would have a field day with a story like this. So as paranoia scooted through town, the threats poured in, and people passed the word that the impotent Yankee was going to flunk their reason to live. When in truth my husband hadn't yet put a single red mark anywhere near that clown.

That night, Sheriff Owen McCord appeared at our kitchen door, hunched under the porch light like a hungry armadillo, his pointy face exaggerated by shadow.

Matthew was glad that the strong arm of the law had finally

come over to offer its support. Owen, without so much as a smile, asked him to step outside to talk. It didn't look good, but I learned long ago to let men swerve through their own peculiar curves. And so I washed up the dishes and waited.

A few minutes passed, and then Matthew rushed in and locked the door behind him. His hair was messed up, and his shirt was ripped at the collar.

"What the hell happened?"

The phone started ringing.

"Forget about it," he said, tromping out of the kitchen.

"Honey?" I yanked up the phone. "Hello?"

"And I stood upon the sand of the sea," a young man's voice rasped, "and I saw a beast rise up . . ." I slammed the receiver down and followed Matthew up the stairs and into our bedroom.

He was bucking around in the closet, more rankled than I had ever seen him. Hangers scraped along the cedar rods. Shoeboxes tumbled to the floor.

"Honey," I said. "What happened?"

He emerged from the closet with a rifle in one hand and a pistol in the other. "Bradley!" he shouted.

"Now, what are you going to do with those?" I said.

"Don't worry, Ginny," he said. "Bradley, come up here a minute!"

"Matt, stop this. Whatever you're doing, just stop it." The phone on our nightstand let out its soft purr, now suddenly menacing. After three rings it stopped. "That kid better notta picked up that phone," I said.

Matthew put the guns on the bed and pulled off his torn shirt. "Some deputy came out from behind your car," he said. "He grabbed me, and that brain-injury victim we have for a sheriff told me to pass that boy or they'll be looking the other way when something happens."

"What did you do?"

He turned and pulled a clean T-shirt out of his dresser drawer. "I told him to blow me."

"What?" I couldn't believe it. "What did you do that for?"

He slipped his shirt over his narrow shoulders. "Then he got me in a headlock and told me to say uncle."

Who would have thought that Jimmy Carter would have grown up to be such a lightning rod? I remembered seeing his little butt shine that bench in Pop Warner, and then for sure he made strides in junior high. But nobody expected him to become the best athlete to come out of this region since Troy Aikman, and the only white boy to run a 4.3 forty in the entire state of Texas. When you combine that with the fact that he's dumber than a Hershey bar, well, then you've got trouble.

"The kid reads at a third-grade level," Matthew said, tucking his shirt in. "He couldn't tell you the chemical equation for water."

There was a knock at the bedroom door. Bradley leaned into the room and said, "Mom? Dad? Some guy said he's on his way over. He said . . ."

"I don't want to hear it," I snapped.

"Mom, he told me we should leave the house, now!"

Matthew picked up the guns and said, "Come over here, son. Sit down."

Bradley moved with that surprising grace of his and sat at the end of the bed.

"I just want to say something to both of you," Matthew said. The guns were pointed down at our new carpet. "I didn't see this coming, and I'm sorry for that. But there's right and there's wrong. Every species has its protocol."

"Yeah," I said. "Survival, Matthew."

"Ginny," he said. "That's what I'm talking about." He turned away from me and looked down at Bradley. "We're looking at right and wrong, son. And yes, family and safety too. But we're also looking at human destiny and opportunity."

"We're looking at Jimmy Carter running a toss sweep," I shouted, "or a slab of lime with your name on it, and maybe ours too."

"Dad?" Bradley said, his soft voice startling in its contrast to mine. "Why don't you just pass him? I'll get to start next year, and Bailey and Joe will start talking to me again."

"This isn't about you, Bradley," Matthew said. "Is that what you think? That I'm not going to pass him so you can play more?"

"No, not really," Bradley said. "But people are talking like that."

"Goddammit, Matthew!" I said. "It is so about him, and it's about me too. The boy's lost his friends. His teammates won't even play with him. We can't sleep at night because we don't feel safe in our own house!"

"Please, Dad!" Bradley said. "Just pass that stupid bastard."

My husband looked from his son to me, as if he were suddenly deaf, his eyes reaching out to communicate, to express what his words couldn't. He had been betrayed by everyone—the law, his friends and neighbors, and now his family. If I weren't so mad at his pigheadedness I would have felt the sting he must have felt.

"A man," he said, as if he was speaking to himself. "Don't you get it? We have evolved, the engine working so hard to get us on two legs. It's a man's job, a man's duty, to stay upright."

Matthew, with the guns pulling down at him, a Wild West outlaw defeated, wrangled in by the posse we had become, looked at me so surprised that I couldn't say anything. He took in a deep breath, and looked out the window, defiantly. "Well," he said. "If they're on their way over here, we better get prepared." He handed the pistol to Bradley, letting it fall from his bent index finger into Bradley's open hand.

"I don't want to shoot anybody," Bradley said.

"Goddammit, Matt," I said. "Would you look at this? This is crazy!"

"What do you want me to do, honey?" he said. "Cars are circling the neighborhood."

"I want you to announce to the world that you're passing that boy, right now! This is ridiculous."

"I don't know if I can do that."

"Fine," I said, picking up the phone. "Then I'll do it."

It was Tuesday night. Grades were due on Wednesday, and the first game of the state playoffs was Friday.

"Hello, Margie?" I said into the phone.

"Yes?"

"Margie, this is Ginny. Will you be a dear and call everyone you know and just pass the word that Jimmy will take the field Friday night?"

The second I hung up, the phone rang. I picked it up. "Hello?"

A man said, "You better be ready, cuz nobody's safe."

"Jesus." I jammed the receiver into its cradle and said, "Bradley, when the phone rings, answer it. Don't say hello. Say he's playing. He aced the test."

As Bradley left the room, the phone started ringing. I looked over at Matthew as he turned away from me, his body slumping into the closet. I could hear Bradley down the hallway, lying into the phone. "No," he was saying. "I'm not kidding."

For the rest of the evening Matthew moped around the house, not talking to anyone. All night long he crawled in and out of bed. I listened to his defeated footfalls, wondering about a man's heart, its mysterious do-si-do. How could he not see that he was hurting his family? And this kid, the brainless idol, what would any of this matter to him? He would find some college that would look the other way, and he'd inevitably go from Friday-night messiah to Saturday-afternoon god whether Matthew passed him or not.

When I got up the next morning, Matthew was gone. The house, bought just two years ago after we sold the dude ranch Dad had left us, felt like an empty warehouse. Bradley, slopping corn puffs into his mouth, one spoonful after another, was finishing up some trig homework.

"What's wrong?" he asked.

I filled the coffeepot at the faucet and looked out the window. The morning sun glinted off the cookie-cutter houses of our neighborhood, a postcard of the mundane.

"I couldn't sleep," I said.

"Neither could Dad. He came into my room at about four o'clock and sat beside my bed and watched me fake sleep." He jammed a spoonful of cereal into his mouth. "But then I opened my eyes and said, 'Hey, Dad.'"

"Don't talk with your mouth full."

"The moon was bright last night."

"It's almost full," I said, pouring the water into the coffee maker.

"Dad was even weirder than usual."

"Bradley, don't say that."

He took a sip of juice and said, "He was talking about, like, the moon's gravitational pull, like the tides and stuff."

I pressed the On switch and pulled a cup out of the cupboard, hoping that this coffee would take away my headache.

"And he just went off, you know how he does, about how the force between the earth and the moon doesn't match up along the line between their centers, or something, and how that produces a torque on the earth and how it somehow accelerates the moon. I don't know. I just let him talk."

The coffeemaker percolated, sending a clear liquid into the pot.

"Shit," I said. I'd forgotten to put coffee into the filter.

That day everything was normal again. Bradley's friends ate lunch with him. Matthew's students raised their hands before speaking. Anger turned into excitement. The game against Odessa Central was only two days away.

But here's the thing: Matthew went into his office that morning, disillusioned and sleep deprived, and he looked at the picture of the clown pointing at him, and he flunked that boy. As my daddy used to say, "God bless the man foolish enough to do what's right."

Matthew went to Graham's office with his final grades. He'd placed the picture of the clown on top, with the small *F* in red on the bottom right-hand corner.

Graham, his only true friend—and the man I'd secretly known for the past two years in the shadows of the Days Inn—shook his head in that controlled way of his. "This doesn't matter," he said. "I'll just override it."

Matthew moved to the door. "I'm sure the Odessa press would love to hear about that."

"Matthew!" Graham said.

"Can't build a house," my husband said, "on quicksand."

"Okay, look," Graham said. "Would it make any difference if I told you the boy lost his mother this summer? I mean, the kid's an orphan, for Christ's sake. Would it make a difference if I told you he was living in foster care?"

"I know that," Matthew said. "Everybody knows that."

"So will you think about it?" Graham said. "Please just think about what you're doing here. Football is all this kid's got."

"That's no reason to pass someone," Matthew said, shaking his head. "I'll be willing to stay after school to tutor him and to help him pick his grades up. But I won't be passing him if he doesn't earn it."

That afternoon, in room 314, the drapes pulled against the traffic on Tulane Avenue, Graham and I started in on our Wednesday-afternoon ritual. We always tried to get room 314 because we had drunkenly stumbled into each other on March 14 at a faculty party both my husband and Graham's wife couldn't attend. Things lead to other things, what can I say?

He was a venturesome, confident lover, and I found myself thinking about him Tuesday nights while stirring the noodles or washing the dishes. But when he showed up fifteen minutes late, he was distant and angry. I lay on the bed in my new bra and panties, which he failed to notice.

"What's wrong?"

He started taking his clothes off. "I don't want to talk about it."

"How male of you."

"I don't get it, Ginny. What do you see in him?"

"Who?"

He turned away from me and unzipped his pants. "You know who." He stripped down to his briefs and paced the room, telling me what Matt had done.

I couldn't believe it. "Listen, I'm sorry, Graham. I thought he was going to pass him."

"I don't get it," he said. "What's it matter to him? Why does he care so much? Just look the other way. The kid's got a future, and it's not in science, so who cares?"

He pulled his T-shirt off and threw it on the chair beside the dresser. "I mean, at least for me, you know? As a favor to me, after all the times I defended that stupid son-of-a-bitch. Putting my job on the line for him! I know why he did it. Everybody knows. And with Bradley in there we don't have a chance. I mean, with all due respect, Bradley's just, well, he's not Jimmy."

He took a deep breath and ran his hand through his hair. "Oh, man." He shook his head and then turned to a brown paper bag on the dresser behind him and pulled out a bottle of Scotch. "I forgot the glass," he mumbled, before heading into the bathroom.

I climbed off the bed and started putting on my clothes.

He came back into the room, pouring Scotch into the glass. "What are you doing?" he said.

I buttoned my blouse and squirmed into my jeans.

"Oh, God." He set the Scotch on the nightstand. "So, what," he said. "You're leaving?"

I sat on the end of the bed and started putting my shoes on. My white, Easy Spirit walking shoes that Matthew got me so I could take up walking at the mall, or on nice days in the park, which is where he thought I was right now.

Graham crawled onto the bed behind me. "Ginny," he said, trying to get hold of my arm. "Don't go. Come on."

"Don't touch me." I stood up and moved away from him with a shoe still in my hand. I grabbed my purse and pulled open the door, pointing the shoe at him. "And don't you ever speak about my family like that. You hear me? Ever."

The next day the news broke that a science teacher had done what no defense in the state of Texas could do: stop the Ambrose offense dead in its tracks. El Presidenté had been deposed, and our kindhearted son was stepping in.

Coach Stubbe was furious, and he took it out on Bradley, making him run laps that Thursday afternoon during practice. Then he had him do the stairs and several wind sprints while the other boys stood and watched, their shoulders hunched glumly. Their season was over, they knew it. Those ranch boys from Odessa were going to roll over them.

As Bradley ran himself ragged, Matthew went about his business, as if nothing had changed. He sat in his den preparing lesson plans while cars cruised slowly past the house. With the phone off the hook and most of the lights off, I sat in the kitchen wondering how I'd landed in this spot. Why did I marry an outsider and move back inside? Why did I always try to fit a square into a circle?

The next night the entire town of Ambrose squeezed dejectedly into Ratliff Stadium. The threats had stopped, and now resigned to the fact that what's done is done, people treated us as if we didn't exist. Matthew was determined to go to the game and watch his son play, saying he was "going in upright and coming home upright." We marched in with the throng of Eagles cursing under their breath.

The team took the field with an attempt at the usual fanfare. Bradley swaggered around the gridiron, hiding his exhaustion and fear. He had thick bands of tape around his wrists and his blue and gray uniform seemed to fit better than before, and I must say pride rose up in me at the sight of the new starting tailback.

As our boys did their stretches, and Bobby Lee Green, the first black quarterback to ever start for Ambrose tossed the ball to that lanky Edwards boy on the sidelines, those Odessa boys lumbered onto the field, their marching band shrieking and pounding the stands like elephants. They were impressive. Their fresh red and white uniforms seemed to bound with every movement. It was pure religious fervor, and those found souls across the field stomped and clapped with the fire of the newly converted.

Coach Stubbe and his assistants crossed their arms over the clipboards on their chests. Mr. Cluster, the mixed-breed, homosexual bandleader, raised his arms and stared into the chatty horde of teenagers before him. They quieted instantly and as his arms whipped down they dove headlong into an almost unrecognizable rendition of "Tequila." The students rose to their feet and started clapping in time.

Matthew and I watched from the nosebleed seats, second-to-last row, behind everybody. I scanned the crowd below and spotted Graham sitting beside Doris, his paunchy wife, who shoved popcorn into her mouth. Matthew was glowing. His eyes followed our son who was making quick cuts, testing the turf. Heads turned in our direction. Matthew looked right over them, enjoying what he'd come here for. And me, not knowing my husband as well as I should, couldn't tell if the motor in him was on high gear working hard to ignore the fanatics around him, or if he was simply beyond their small-minded longings. As I looked at him, I felt ashamed of my ignorance. Being with somebody is like taking a class, and I had been a student in this subject for almost twenty years and my grade was no better than that dim-witted jock who got us into this mess.

"What are you looking at?" Matthew said. "If I didn't know any better, I'd say you're like all of them, staring at me."

"Is that what you think?"

"You know what I think?" he said. "I've been thinking a lot lately. And it's funny, actually." He puffed out a pathetic chuckle. "I think I did all this for you. For us, maybe."

The captains jogged to the middle of the field for the coin toss.

"What?" I said.

"It didn't really work, though, did it?" he whispered.

The coin flashed silver in the stadium lights, and the Odessa boys started jumping around.

Matt looked out over the crowd and said, "You were only months, maybe weeks away from leaving me, weren't you? Or from kicking me out. I had nothing to lose."

The kickoff team took the field, Bradley on the far end, his taped wrists gleaming under the lights. All of Ambrose rose to their feet, excitement finally bubbling up against their will, hope's inexhaustible legs still moving forward.

"Don't deny it," he said, watching his son crouch in front of the Odessa sidelines. "I probably wouldn't have blamed you. But hey, this whole thing provided us with a little excitement, if nothing else."

That short Mexican boy, Arthur Duarte, laid his foot on the ball so hard it sailed nearly seventy-five yards and almost hit the goalpost.

"But now you probably resent me even more than you did before," he said.

"Give me a break," I said, trying to assemble some logic in my caught-off-guard head.

The defense huddled at the twenty-yard line, Bradley at free safety. We were still on our feet.

"I don't believe you," I said. "You would have done it exactly the same with or without me."

"I'm a male of the species," he said, and then cupped his hands around his mouth. "Come on, Bradley!" he shouted. "Our concept of right and wrong is predicated on our desire to survive."

"Oh, God," I said. "Do you have to talk science now?"

The defense broke its huddle, and Bradley crouched behind the middle linebacker, a sign of the "blue-dog blitz," where the two middle linebackers fake up and then my son shoots through the line uncontested, usually sacking the quarterback for a ten-yard loss. But the Odessa boys knew what was coming, and they picked up Bradley with the fullback. Their speedy little black receiver ran right down the middle of the field, right where Bradley would have been if he hadn't blitzed. The quarterback let the ball fly, and that beautiful spiral bounced on the turf twenty yards beyond the wide-open black boy, who stormed back to the huddle, his hands flapping all around his body.

"I wanted to teach my son," Matthew said, "to do what's right. And, I wanted to show you that I wasn't as feeble as you thought."

"Matt." This was all I could think to say.

"It was the right thing to do, I'm sure of it, but you'd underestimate me if you didn't think it was also expedient."

"Heaven forbid I'd underestimate you," I said, letting my sarcasm do the work I was too lazy to do.

The Odessa offense chipped away, gaining four yards here, six yards there, until they were finally stopped on the sixteen-yard line. They kicked a field goal. A collective sigh of relief filled the stands as the Odessa special teams took the field.

It was only 3–0, and our offense readied itself on the sidelines. Watching my boy out there had always been difficult. When he played defense, it wasn't so bad, as he was doing the hitting. But I couldn't stand to see my boy put his hands on that football.

When our offense lined up in an I formation, and when that tubby Lancaster boy hiked the ball, Bobby Lee Green tossed it to Bradley on a sweep to the weak side. Here's the thing, though: those huge overweight mongrels on our offensive line barely moved, letting the defense smother my boy for a four-yard loss. Bradley rose from the pile and rushed back to the huddle, clapping his hands. There were more disgruntled faces snarling up at us. The next play: same thing, other side. It was now third down and sixteen on our twelve-yard line. Bradley kept rushing and clapping, like nothing unusual was happening. The team was conspiring against my boy, and there he was acting just like his father.

"They're gonna let him get killed," I said.

"He'll keep fighting," Matthew said, not noticing the pissed-off faces, cursing us—Parnell Owens, Mr. and Mrs. McCloud, the Malones, people once our friends.

"You're as stupid as a dead mule," I said.

"I told you," he said. "We do this for you."

"Don't give me that shit," I said, trying to watch the next play.

Bobby Lee Green faded back and whipped a flair pass to my boy out in the flat. Two Odessa linebackers pummeled him like he was a bag of feed.

"Goddammit! Start blocking!" I hollered. More faces—the Bledsoes, Jane Walters, Nellie O'Neill.

"This is ridiculous," I said. "I want you to go get him so we can leave. This whole town can just go to hell." I almost started crying, I was so upset, everything finally brimming to the surface. This was my hometown, and they were shitting on me and my family.

Matt actually put his arm around me. "It'll be okay, honey. You're always a little afraid when he plays."

Our punter stood in the endzone, his hands stretched out in front of him, waiting for the ball. Bradley paced the sidelines, his hands on his hips, ready to play defense.

"It's interesting though," Matthew said, "how you've never missed a game."

"So?" I said.

"Well, if he didn't keep fighting, there'd probably be something inside you that wouldn't forgive him."

"Bullshit," I said. "Now go do something. He's limping."

"This is his game, honey." Matthew said this with a loveliness that shocked me. "Just relax and watch our boy." He pulled me into his shoulder as the defense fanned onto the field.

I was angry with my husband, an anger that had been hanging around for so long I now took it for granted. But standing there, I wondered where the anger had come from. He had not hurt me. He had simply drifted away from my drifting, like we had been caught in two divergent currents.

As our son shot through the pulling guard and tackle to bring the Odessa running back to the ground, I looked at my husband and said, "I don't care what you say. This is crazy."

"Maybe so," he said. "But the kid's not giving up."

For a moment I wondered who he was talking about. In college, he would call himself "the Kid," as in "The Kid aced the exam," or "The Kid's going on a road trip to Montana."

The rest of the half was more of the same—the offensive line playing patty-cakes with the Odessa defense, Bradley getting crushed, jumping to his feet, rushing back to the huddle.

But the defense kept them in the game and at halftime the score was Odessa 13, Ambrose 0.

Odessa's red and white band marched onto the field, tooting out a pop song that sounded vaguely familiar.

"I gotta go to the ladies' room," I said.

Matthew was looking up at the moon in the clear sky. "Did you know that the moon is slipping away from us? Every year it takes a little longer to circle the earth, moving farther and farther away. It's imperceptible."

"Really?" I said.

He nodded and scanned the crowd for the first time.

"Matt, I really do have to go to the restroom."

"Oh, I'm sorry," he said moving out of the way. "Say hi to Graham for me. I mean, if you see him." He threw a sideways glance my way. "I mean, you intend to see him again, don't you?"

This was our personal gridiron. I could see it now. He had set this up, a head-to-head showdown in a hostile environment. He had just flattened me.

"You don't want to escort me?" I said, ignoring his question.

"I don't have to go. But if you want me to . . ."

"Don't bother," I said, scooting past him and down the stairs.

In the bathroom Patsy Welch stood in front of a mirror, fluffing her hair with her fingers.

A stall opened. Juanita Huldice scurried out and gawked at me through her large rimless glasses.

"What are you looking at?" I said.

She hobbled by me and left the restroom without even washing her hands. Patsy turned from the mirror and came toward me. I stood firm, ready to fight. She reached up and placed her hand on my shoulder like the schoolteacher she is.

"Not all of us," she said, and then winked at me. "This'll be forgotten by Christmas."

"Are you kidding?" I said, knowing that as time passes the fish gets bigger, the snow deeper.

Matthew ignored me as I came up the steps toward him. The Ambrose marching band roamed the field with all the precision of overmedicated geriatrics. As they meandered off the field, followed by those awkward flag girls, something happened, something that will not likely be replaced in West Texas lore anytime soon. Our boys took the field, but this time it was a bit different. This time they bounded out of that dark hallway with an uncontrollable excitement, as if the Odessa boys hadn't just walked all over them for twenty-four minutes.

They charged their sideline with long, wild strides and beside them, in his low-hanging Dickies and Tommy Hilfiger sweatshirt, was El Presidenté himself, Jimmy Carter, the boy who for weeks juked and spun through our dreams, shaking us free of all the tackles we had endured throughout our lives.

When they huddled together, Jimmy was saying something to them, exhorting them with those charming one-syllable grunts he had mastered in his twelve years of education.

The Odessa team still hadn't taken the field, and for these moments it felt like an earlier time, before the crash-and-burn this situation had become. Jimmy moved through the huddle, slapping the blue and gray helmets of his teammates, and then he jogged across the track and came into the stands. The mob of shrieking fans reached out their hands to him and he touched them as he scanned the crowd and ascended the steps. The band, straggling into the stands, had stopped moving. People couldn't take their eyes off the boy. He caught my husband's eye and started taking the steps two at a time, heading up to the heights of the stadium. His mouth was closed, with a seriousness never seen on that shiny face. He reached our row and stood in the aisle, staring at my husband.

"Well, hello, Jimmy," Matthew said, as if the boy had just walked into his office at school.

"Sir?" Jimmy said. "I want to apologize for what I did."

"You didn't do anything, Jimmy."

"You must think I'm stupid," Jimmy said with a smile.

"No, I don't, Jimmy."

"Well, I'll be in class on Monday with my homework done."

"That'll be fine," my husband said.

Jimmy stuck out his perfectly formed hand. "I'm sorry, sir."

My husband took the boy's hand and said, "Apology accepted."

Jimmy turned and looked at the town of Ambrose below him and out at the team on the field. "Boy howdy!" he shouted. "Let's kick some ass!"

The crowd looked around, bewildered. They needed time to process this conundrum—their savior embracing their enemy. But once he made it back down to the field repeatedly hurling his arms into the air, the throng of people below let loose with the chants of the saved, Joshua fit the battle of Jericho, and all that. The band blew its horns. The offensive line started blocking, and my exhausted, battered boy carried the team to a 26–20 defeat.

The fans—our neighbors and acquaintances, Matt's present and past students—left the stadium as exhausted as the team, congratulating us for raising such a fine boy. "Almost got'r done tonight," Harvey Walters said. "Almost got'r done."

"There's always next year," someone hollered.

That night I woke up alone in our bed. It was a little after three and the house was so still it felt like it was waiting for something. I had been dreaming, but for the life of me I couldn't remember the chaos in my head. Matthew's clothes, rumpled with the memory of his body, were bunched on the chair in the corner. The top drawer of his dresser hung open, and the closet door was cracked. It seemed like everything in the room was leaning toward me.

My feet found the floor, and then I was in the hallway heading toward my son's bedroom. He was lying on his back, huffing the shallow breath that bruised ribs bring, and my husband was slumped in the chair beside him, his tattered bathrobe half open.

I crept into the room, and watched Matthew as I inched my way around the bed. His face was turned towards the window. The light of the moon ran across his forehead and cheekbone. He seemed so peaceful, sleeping by his son. I didn't want to wake him and subject him to all the disappointment I brought with me. So I stood there and looked at him, this quiet, oddly passionate northerner I stuck my claim into so many years ago, this man who could still surprise me, showing me things I didn't even know I wanted to see, and still despite it all, fighting for something I thought we'd given up on years ago.

I traced the light from his face through the window, to its source. The moon hung there in the dark sky, all alone.

It's slipping away, he'd said, so slowly you can't even notice.

I put my hand on his shoulder. I wanted to shake him. "Honey," I said. "Honey, wake up." I wanted him to open his eyes and see me, still here, beside him.

He stirred and then squinted up at me in the darkness.

"Hey," I said.

"Hey." He shook his head and cleared his throat. "What are you doing up so late?"

I didn't know what to say. I couldn't think of a single word.

He said, "Is everything okay?"

I nodded and leaned into him, my body pressing against his.

"What's wrong, honey?" he whispered.

I touched his messy hair and pulled his head into my chest. I could feel his resistance, but then something happened, his body relaxed, as if he'd suddenly released a long, deep breath.

"That was something, wasn't it?" he said.

I could feel his arms rise up and wrap around me like some forgotten joy. "Yes," I said. "Yes, it was."

King of America

I hang for my father. I hang for what I can't remember. And what I can. I hang for the foot my mother found, bloody, in the mangrove tree. Mother said the Vietcong did it to scare us, to stop us from running. She found his arm two days later in the palm fronds. It was his arm, she knew, from the mark of a bullet that had grazed him in the war, a bit of scar tissue on the inside of his forearm. Besides the picture I carry everywhere, this is what I remember of my father: an arm here, a leg there.

I live in Vegas now. Everything is lights here. So much light the stars refuse to shine. And the wind, it pushes on windows until they moan. It never stops. Wind and lights all day and night. The slots ping and whir below me. They make noise when they're angry. They scream and howl. Old people are plugged in to the machines. Little chains connect their hearts to diamonds and cherries.

. . .

In our small village on the Mekong River my father was known as an organizer. He hid boats in the reeds and guided people out to the bay in darkness, paddling at night through gunfire. My mother said the wind told them he was the one. And one day he went from human being to anatomy. They called him an agitator. But he was just a farmer who wanted freedom, who made up love poems to my mother. In the reeducation camp he wrote poems on little scraps of paper, poems about birds and the sky. They found them and burned them, and then punished him with isolation. But he remembered in his head. He would say them to me when I lay down to sleep.

Now, seven days a week except Wednesday, I am lowered from the ceiling to "Louie, Louie." Every hour on the hour it is Mardi Gras for twenty minutes. There is a main stage where singers sing and dancers dance. A float goes around the room on rails, hanging from the ceiling. Girls dance on the float in colorful costumes with fruit on their heads. They throw beads to the people below. Then there is Bobby and me, hanging from cables above the casino floor. We dance and lipsync in midair. We are the later King, in all-white jumpsuits, rhinestones, sunglasses and sideburns. Bobby wears a wig. I use my real hair. Bobby hangs ten feet away, facing me. He doesn't curl his lip. *They can't even see our faces,* he says. I curl my lip. Before the music starts we are on a platform on the ceiling. It is dark. *You ready, gookface?* Bobby says. The music starts. I can feel the ceiling shake into the soles of my feet. And then it slides open and we are lowered above the people who sit at slot machines and blackjack tables, cigarettes in their mouths, large plastic cups in their hands.

• • •

After they killed my father, the fleeing stopped. For a time, anyhow. Two years passed. I was nine years old. My mother cried and whispered to me to be strong. And then she told me a story. It was during the war, she said. My father was a brave soldier. He didn't like American GIs and they didn't like him. But sometimes they had to fight side by side. My mother moved her sleeping pad and showed it to me. *This,* she said, *was a gift from an American to your father.* Something was wrong because she cried again. *This is yours,* she said. *Keep it. Don't let go.* In my hands she placed the King.

Above the crowd we dance to "Love Shack." Bobby doesn't even move his hips. He says everyone is watching the fruit. He says he's eaten the entire float. He says Miss Strawberry liked his big banana. And then he laughs. There is strawberry, pineapple, watermelon, a slice of lemon and lime, a coconut, and mango. Lynh is mango. She is the most beautiful mango. Even with her chest made bigger. *Big mangoes,* Bobby says. I speak Viet with her. But she sneers at me. *We're in America now, dumbass! Speak American!* Lynh is someone I could love. Underneath she is sweet. I can see it when she looks at herself in the mirror. There is softness in her eyes. Other fruit are nice. But Lynh is from Vietnam, and Mother would be happy about that. Bobby says he ate mango too. He says mango was the sweetest.

My mother told the story of how the GI saved my father's life. He carried Father for miles on his back through the forest and bullets flying. Somehow my father found him later and gave the GI several *taels* of gold, from trinkets and jewelry he had found or stolen. The GI told him to stay there, and he went away. *He came back later with this,* my mother said, pointing at the record cover. *He gave it to your father and said this is the King. If you want to know where I come from listen to this.* And then she told me that we could never listen in Vietnam. But that someday soon I would be able to listen. Then one day Mother said Grandma was sick in the district hospital in Thong Nhat near Ho Nai City. I was to stay with Uncle while she went to visit. *Take this,* she said. Her fingers touched the record of the King. His lip was curled, his collar turned up. *Take this with you,* she said.

In the green room, after the first show, Lynh is nowhere. Tracy (strawberry) and Pam (lemon) are eating crackers and talking about the soap opera that plays on the TV. *Where's Lynh?* I ask. *I don't know, Cowboy.* Pam calls everyone Cowboy. The green room is where we wait for the next show. I don't know why it is called green. The walls are pink. A large mirror is on one wall. My hair is big and combed back. My sideburns look real. Glue holds them down. Sometimes Lynh helps me put them on. Her fingers touch my face like meditation. Her fingers become the whole world. It is then that I tell her how much I practice, alone in front of the mirror for hours, trying to get my voice deep enough. It is then that I tell her of my dream to get out of this place, and play the biggest stages on the strip, to be the best King in Vegas.

I stayed with my uncle for two weeks when everything changed. One night he woke me from a very deep sleep. *Come on,* he whispered. *We are leaving now.* He told me to be quiet, to crawl behind him to the banks of the river. *Your aunt and cousins will be waiting for us.* I grabbed the record and pushed it under my shirt. It was a windy night, and the trees were bending. I crawled through the wind and the darkness. My uncle kept low and moved fast like an animal. Coconuts fell from the sky, pounding on the ground around us. We crawled until we got to rows and rows of willow trees that were whipping and hissing in the wind. A dark cloud moved overhead, and rain began to fall. There were many people crawling to the banks of the river. Wind pushed the water, slapping the shore and the sides of the boat. My uncle held the boat while we climbed in. My aunt was already on board and my cousins Phuoc and Mai were pushed up against the barrels of fuel in the small engine room. More and more people climbed on. Water was rising.

Lynh is a sad girl. The curse words that come from her mouth, her smart comments, these are just the armor she wears. She was on a boat, too. But she only tells part of her story. Once they land in Hong Kong, she stops, and her eyes turn down. And then she talks about San Jose. Maybe one day she will tell me. Stories are told down at Xinh Xinh Restaurant, stories about rape and starvation in those camps in Hong Kong. Vo and Huong tell of the separation of men and women and how they were forced to stay in their tents for days on end, starving with other men, not knowing what was happening to the girls, and that was the worst thing, they say. But I don't want to think about that. Not until Lynh tells me what happened to her, then I will listen and be strong. I want to marry Lynh. I want to take her to Xinh Xinh Restaurant one night and order her the number 92 special with Cari Tom and a spring roll. I will invite all of our friends and they will be in the kitchen waiting for me to get down on my knee. And then we will clear out the tables and we will dance. There is not a woman more beautiful than Lynh. We will be married at Our Lady of La Vang on a Sunday afternoon. And while we say our vows, the wind will quiet down. From that day on she will no longer need to dance in casinos. She will only dance for me.

We tried to push the boat out. It wouldn't move. So many people pushing it down into the sand. My uncle ordered men out. They refused. My uncle pulled out a gun and pointed it at them. Rain was coming down. Two men climbed out, and then two more. They helped push us out of the sand and into the river, and then they tried to climb back on. There were already too many people, but my uncle knew we could not fight. The guard would hear us and start shooting.

The next show is going to start in a half hour. Bobby is nowhere. I chew on a crab leg and practice a dance move. I ask Lynnette (pineapple) if she's seen Lynh. *Oh, yeah, sweetie. She was running out to the parking lot. Bobby was chasing after her,* she says. *They were really going at it.* The hallways are long here. Bobby says the whole city is a maze. We are fucking mice, he says, all racing for the cheese. The hot wind blows on me as I walk out the door. In the far corner of the parking lot, Bobby dressed as the King, with his hands in the air, yells at Lynh, who stands by her car with the mango on her head. A family gets out of their car and points at me as I run across the lot. *Oh Jesus,* Bobby says. *Look who's here!*

The orders were to push the boat out past the National Guard post a hundred meters down the river. Once quietly past, the engine would be started, and hopefully we'd make it out to the bay and to freedom. But the wind was angry, and the rain fell hard. Men pushed poles into the river's sandy bottom, but we weren't moving. We were out in the middle of the river for a long time. The wind did not let up. Uncle wanted to turn the boat around and go back to the shore. Maybe try again later. But then a light, a bright light moved across the river and stopped on our boat. *Start the engine,* Uncle shouted. *Start the engine!*

Lynh is crying. Dark tears run down her face. I ask if she is okay. Bobby tells me he will pound my sushi head if I don't leave. The sun is very hot, and the wind dries everything up. *What is going on, Lynh?* I say in Viet. She tells me that there was a red line this morning, and then she did it again and another red line appeared, and Bobby is probably the reason. *What the hell did you say to her?* Bobby asks.

Uncle got to the engine room, and Hoa was wrapping a cord around the engine wheel. *What happened?* Uncle screamed. Hoa's fingers shook as he struggled with the cord. *Phuoc wrapped it the wrong way,* Hoa said. Uncle pushed Hoa back and pulled on the cord. The engine sputtered and popped, and then it started. Guns exploded all around us. Red bullets scraped the wind. *Everybody down!* Uncle shouted. *Khanh, turn the boat to the west! No, too many rocks, keep straight. Straight!*

That baby ain't mine, Bobby says. *Could be any crackhead dealer in this town for all you know.* Lynh looks at Bobby so angry and then she goes at him, the mango on her head crashing into him, her fingernails tearing at his face and neck. Bobby tries to hold her off. I don't know why, but I pull her away. Her arms and legs flap like a bird. I push her back against her car. *Fucking bitch!* Bobby says. *I gotta fucking show to do.* Bobby straightens the wig on his balding head. A small crowd has gathered. An old couple, a few college-age boys, and the family that saw me run across the parking lot. *Can you believe this?* Bobby says, looking around at the strangers.

We were moving down the river, and the gunshots were fading now. Soon all we could hear was the engine and the knocking of water on the sides of the boat. As we moved out into the bay and then into the wide ocean, a storm came down on us. Water splashed into the boat. Uncle got sick into the water that was around my ankles. Many others got sick. We started bailing out the vomit and water. The pump was not getting it all out. Some used cups and buckets. I used my hands. In the water I saw blood. Uncle told us to keep bailing, and then he passed out. Kanh saw the blood in the water and crawled up the boat. Two men had been hit by gunfire, and they were dead. A woman was screaming and crying. Kanh touched the neck of one of the dead men and then lifted him up and pushed him overboard. The woman's little fists pounded on Kanh's back. He turned and touched the other man's neck, and then he got sick. Kanh crossed himself and said a prayer, and then he pushed the man's body into the raging sea.

Bobby holds the wig down on his head. The wind is trying to push it off. He takes a deep breath and says something that surprises me. He is almost tender. *Let's talk about this later, okay? Okay, Lynh?* He reaches out and touches Lynh's wrist. She slaps at him and screams. I pull her away from him. *Goddammit,* Bobby says. *Fucking boat people.* He turns to the crowd that is watching us. *They're crazy. Fucking nuts.* And then he shakes his head and walks back toward the casino. This is the time for our language. I ask Lynh if she is okay. She says, *I want to have this baby.* I ask her why. She shakes her head and says, *I don't know.* Many of us came here like broken bamboo, without roots, splintered. She says she doesn't care who the father is. She just wants something that is her own.

Black walls of water, rising and falling. That was all you could see. All night long. When morning came the sun was shining and the sea was flat. The engine room smelled of diesel fuel and vomit and urine. The engine growled, and most of us were too sick to eat. Later that morning dolphins started swimming beside the boat. In Vietnam it is said that dolphins bring good luck. I saw smiles for the first time. My older cousin, Phuoc, held his hand out and almost touched one. Uncle slept late, but when he awoke he shouted at Kanh for steering us to the south toward Con Son Island, the most eastern part of Vietnam, a place where many were imprisoned. Uncle took over and set us on course due east. Eventually the dolphins left us alone and we moved on for two days across calm seas.

I will help you, I say to Lynh. The strangers are moving away now. *Tomorrow I try for better jobs, on the strip. I'll make a lot more money.* Air comes out of her lips. She shakes her head and opens the door to her car and gets in. *You know I love you,* I say. She is crying again. The dark lines on her face filling with salt tears. *You wouldn't say such things, if you really knew me.* She pulls the mango off her head and closes the door. *I know you, Lynh. We come from the same place.* She starts the car and the window comes down. *You look at the future,* she says, *and then when it comes, it doesn't look like you thought it would.* I ask her where she is going. *For a drive,* she says, *away from here,* and I get the feeling I may never see her again. She might drive away forever. She has secrets. Secrets that push her away from love like the waves that night that pushed me from my home. *Lynh,* I say. *I will help you. I will raise the child up like it is my own. I will be a good father.* Her hand reaches out of the window and touches my knuckles.

My uncle was very sick. And many others were too. For several days our motor pushed us east, and we were running out of food and water. I was dizzy from hunger, my head and stomach aching.

Uncle asked me one morning if I had prayed. I told him I prayed many times. He said that nothing makes God so strong as being lost at sea. And then he told me that my father had organized this escape just before he died. He told me that my father was the reason so many were free. And he never did it for money, like many men. My father was a hero, he said, a dreamer whose dreams were too big for Vietnam. Later that morning we spotted a boat in the distance. Kanh and Hoa pulled out their guns and told everyone to stay down. Thai pirates might come and kill us all, they said. Take everything we had. When the boat got closer we grew more frightened. My aunt put her arms around Phuoc and Mai while I kept my eye out the window of the cabin, watching as the boat got bigger and bigger. I had heard stories of pirates, pulling the gold teeth out of a man's head, and then throwing him overboard to be eaten by sharks. There were many stories. On the Thai island of Koh Kra, all the men were killed and their daughters and wives raped.

Lynh drives away from me, into the desert. On Flamingo she turns right, and I lose sight of her. The wind is hot, but so dry you don't sweat. It will blow forever.

We were lucky. They were not pirates, only fishermen. But they had guns, and they were pointing them at us. They were scared, too. But when they saw what they had run into, they put their guns away and tried to tell Kanh something. They were from Malaysia. They pointed and smiled. And then Kanh gave them our guns in exchange for a barrel of fuel. People were angry that he traded the guns. *We need guns!* they shouted. *We are nothing without protection! We need to defend ourselves!*

In the casino I become a rat racing for the cheese. The green room is deserted. Everyone is in their places. I head up the back steps to the ceiling, where Maggie and Ben strap me into my harness. Before the ceiling opens the lights are on. Bobby is ready to go. *She okay, Superman?* he says. Maggie rushes to make sure I am secure. The cords are attached. She gives two good tugs and then runs off to the control booth, where Ben is sitting. The music starts thumping. "Louie, Louie, oh, hoh, we gotta go!" *She's full of shit, Kung Fu,* Bobby says. *You know how many cocks she's sucked, Grasshopper?* The lights click off. It is now pitch-black. In a few seconds the ceiling will slide open, and we will be lowered down into smoke and clapping. But I will not attempt to explain why I do the things I do. Sometimes you do things because they need to be done. It is so dark I cannot see him, but I have seen him in my mind many times, standing there in darkness. And I have also seen what I am about to do. My feet push me backward in my harness. Swinging as high as I can, I tuck my legs up and move towards him at a great speed. As I get close to him his white suit flashes in my mind, and know where his head is.

After several days at sea, an island grew big on the horizon. There was a man on a beach. He was waving at us to come in. As we moved closer, men in uniforms came out onto the sand. When we got to the shallow water, many jumped out of the boat, crying and shouting, crawling onto the shore. The soldiers shouted at us, telling us with their hands to sit down on the sand. One of them spoke French to Kanh. He translated, telling us that we were on a small Malaysian island, and that the soldiers were going to take us to a refugee camp. We got on a bus and went deep into the island behind barbed wire. There was a mound of fire. Kanh told us they were going to burn some of our clothes and belongings for fear of disease and bad smells. They were going to shave the lice off our heads. I still had the King against my stomach. A tall soldier pointed a gun at my uncle and made him take off his clothes, and then he did the same to my aunt and Phuoc and Mai. When he shouted at me, I stepped forward.

The ceiling slides open. Bobby hangs in front of me like a limp, dead king. His eyes are closed and his wig lays back on his head. There is a deep cut across his nose. The music is thumping all around us. My lip is curled, like I trained it, all those hours in front of a mirror. My feet are spread out. My hand is raised in the air. Below us people push their retirement into machines. We are lowered into the smoke that floats above them. People shout up at the fruit float as it moves around the room. Trish (watermelon) throws beaded necklaces down to the people. But now there is no mango. Her platform is empty.

My mother had told me to hold on to the King. She wanted me to remember my father and his dream of taking us to America. So I held him tight against my stomach. But the barrel of the gun was staring me in the face. My legs were shaking. The soldier shouted again and again, until I pulled off my shirt and threw it onto the fire. The soldier looked at the record cover in my hands and asked something. *The King,* I said. He didn't understand. He pointed at the fire. I looked down and saw what the water had done to his face. There was a wisp of black hair, the curled lip, an eyebrow. The rain and the ocean had taken most of him away. As I threw him onto the fire and watched what was left of his face bubble up and disappear, I wondered who he was.

Bobby droops across from me, passed out, slowly waking. Nobody cares. They don't watch us. They are too busy losing their money, or watching the main show, or chasing necklaces. I often wonder what my father would think of me now. I have my own apartment. I send part of my check every month to my mother who lives with my aunt in Thousand Oaks. There are things you should never forget. My father sacrificed everything so I could be here. I throw my right hand up, pointing to the ceiling, mouthing the words to "Louie, Louie." Bobby opens his eyes and looks around. His nose is bleeding. He reaches up and touches the blood, and then looks at his bloody fingers. I twist around and shake my hips. But this is it, tonight is the end of hanging for me. Tomorrow I will audition for booking agents and soon, next week maybe, I will be on a stage at the Mirage or in a lounge at the Luxor. I have worked very hard for this. I have learned every move, every word to every song. Someday people will come from all over to see me. They will buy tickets and get dressed up. They will go out to dinner and then wait in line, excited, talking about what songs I might sing.

During "Love Me Tender" women will throw flowers on the stage. I will pick them up and smell them, lower my sunglasses and wink, and they will scream. There will be groupies who hang out after the show, asking for my autograph, wanting me to sign parts of their anatomy. *Tran Nguyen*, I'll write on a leg extended to me. *King of America*, I'll scribble on a forearm. If there is something I have learned, it is that in this country no dream is too big.

Stories of the Hunt

My father was a hunter who drove a Jeep, and because of this, he was infinitely more exciting than Tim Rutherford's father, who drove a taxi and played darts in a league down at the U-Turn Tavern. And Don Ray Shelton, whose dad wore suits and did something in an office somewhere, always wanted to spend the night at my house so we could watch my dad clean his guns and get ready.

He'd fold up his hunting gear, stuff his backpack, and walk us through the itinerary. "First Mayfield and Dunkirk meet me at the south fork and they hop in the Jeep and we take off up past Devil's Thumb and into the dark and piney, where the road ends and we hike in." It always began like this. The meeting point figured prominently in his stories, and the names of these men I never met. When he'd arrive home a few days later, he'd lug in a head mounted on cedar with the antlers pointing upward. My mother never let such things into the house, so Don Ray Shelton and I would sit up in the attic with a flashlight and poke at their marble eyes and dried tongues.

For some kids it's dinosaurs, for others it's baseball cards or chemistry sets. For me, it was always hunting, deer hunting, and the more interest I showed in it, the more excited my father became, illustrating every facet of the rifle, from cleaning and prepping to loading and aiming.

The summer I turned twelve, my dad, against my mother's wishes, bought me a rifle and took me out to the landfill, where we shot at Coke cans on a big wooden stump in front of a rancid mountain of trash. I was a good shot, most of the time better than Dad.

One night, a school night, later that fall, I overheard my mother talking to him about an upcoming hunting competition near Spokane. She was reading about a cash prize for the biggest buck and a weekend of male gathering. I was shocked to hear her mention my name. "You know what I was thinking?" she said. "What if you took Walt this time?"

"What?" My father sounded annoyed. "Wait a second. You never want him to even touch a gun."

"Well, I think he's old enough now. You know what this would mean to him?"

"Oh, Jesus."

I remember standing outside their bedroom door, my body perfectly still. Once my mom was on my side, I knew I had won. I was finally going to go into the wild with my father. I had spent years trying to win her over, but the funny thing was, Dad kept arguing with her.

Buck's Big Game Journal was a small hunting magazine published two times a year by an old bald guy named Buck MacGuire in Coeur d'Alene, Idaho. It was full of hunting tips, grandiose stories, and pictures—black-and-white photos of various kills and big game caught in outrageous situations. The back page featured the winning photograph, usually some dead moose or elk with its antlers stuck in a tree or a fence. But the one I remember most vividly was of a white-tailed deer tangled up in a clothesline. "Still Alive!" the caption read.

This photo has stayed with me, I think, because of the story I've created behind it. I always imagine that Margaret—my name for her—comes out one evening to get her clothes off the line, when she sees this 175-pound buck kicking and whipping his head. Margaret then runs into the house and gets her husband, Mike, to come out and take a look. Mike goes out and says, "Oh, my God!" and runs back into the house to get a camera, of all things. What people think in such situations astounds me. So he gets the camera and slowly closes in on this wild animal, and before he knows it, Mike has taken the picture that will win him first prize in Buck's annual contest, a picture that will enable Mike and Margaret to finally buy the dryer they always wanted—no more clothesline for them! Here's what the picture looked like: deer antlers, like huge wooden fork tines, rising out of a pair of boxer shorts, and the deer's eyes looking hopelessly towards the camera between flowered panties and two argyle socks.

This is the magazine I subscribed to when I was a kid. It had a circulation of maybe five hundred, and sometimes it came three months late. But it had everything I wanted, and I never threw out a copy. It all ended, however, in the spring of my sixth-grade year, when Buck MacGuire was thrown in prison for unpaid traffic tickets and child pornography. He tried to publish the magazine from his prison cell in Pocatello, but that was futile, and I had to learn to be satisfied with *Field & Stream*.

• • •

Eventually, after several arguments, one ending with my father slamming the garage door, my mother persuaded him to take me to what was actually called the Northwest White-Tailed Deer-Hunting Competition.

"For one weekend, residents of Montana, Idaho, Oregon and Washington will convene just north of Spokane, in the town appropriately called Deer Park, to compete in the biggest shoot-off on the West Coast," it said on the cream-colored brochure.

It was still a month off, but I prepared, shooting as much as I could, and then cleaning my gun—a Savage bolt-action rifle. "The bolt-action rifle," Buck MacGuire wrote, "is more rugged and simple than other rifles, and it is the most accurate rifle on the market." About this, he was right. Dad would make me stand far away or crouch behind trees, and I could still hit the Coke cans.

Dad shot a lot, too, but he never seemed to get any better. "Here," he once said, "give me that gun of yours." He took my gun and started firing at the stump, hitting only one can out of five. "Jesus," he said. "It's getting dark. Let's get home."

My dad worked for Boeing, which in those days meant he'd work a few months and then get laid off and then get rehired. So he'd be there some days when I came home from school. My mother worked all day in a dentist's office, answering the phone and scribbling on a calendar. One day, after school, I found my gun laid out in pieces on my bedroom floor.

"Shit," my dad said. "Like a deer in headlights." He was leaning against the doorframe with a beer in his hand.

I looked at the mess of little gadgets and screws, amazed at all the things inside a rifle. From the outside it looks very simple and basic, but like most things, rifles are deceiving.

"I tell you what, Walt, you put that back together by next weekend and you can go with me."

"But Mom said . . ."

"That you were going, that it's a done deal. Well, I've been thinking about that."

For some reason my father didn't want me to go. But I was too determined to give up, and for the next three days I spent every free minute putting that rifle back together. To the dismay of my father, I had it back in working order two days before we were to leave on our trip. I brought the gun into the living room and set it in his lap.

"What's this?" he said.

"I'm done," I said. "I cleaned every piece, too. It works better now than it ever has."

"Huh," he said. "Well, good, Walt. Now go put it away."

As I moved out of the room, I said, "That's it?"

"What was that?" my dad said. "Walt. You get back in here. What did I say about that, huh? If you got something to say to me, say it to me." He stared at me and then took a drag on his cigarette. "So," he said, leaning back in his chair. "What do you have to say?" Smoke came out of his nose and mouth and hung in the air between us.

"I put my rifle back together," I said.

"The average white-tailed buck weighs one hundred and eighty pounds, although specimens of nearly twice that weight have been shot. It is by far the wariest and most elusive of all big-game animals. The cautious hunter will succeed with the white-tail. Keep the wind in your favor because deer have an exceptional sense of smell." I read Buck MacGuire's hunting tips to my father as we drove over the Cascades that Thursday night. It was dark, so I held a flashlight up to the book.

"You think Buck is going to be there?" my father asked.

"No, Dad. He's in prison, remember?"

"Oh, yeah," he said, shaking his head. "Pervert."

"Yeah," I said. "Sick."

He was quiet for a while. The engine roared as we climbed the mountain, headlights pushing on the dark road ahead of us.

"Look, you're going to want to get some sleep," he said. "Believe me, we've got a shot at winning some of that purse, but only if you get some shut-eye. You've got vision. Just don't lock up and you'll be fine."

"I won't," I said. "If I see a deer, I'll kill it."

"That a boy." He reached over and put his hand on my head. "Now get some sleep."

It was the beginning of November and the Cascades were covered with snow. At one point, I remember waking up and seeing my dad putting chains on the tires. We had another five hours of driving ahead of us and snow on the pass was not going to help. When he got in the Jeep, he said, "Rest those eyes, Walt. And say a prayer for us." He was so tender at that moment that I often wonder if it was a dream. I lay down, resting my head in his lap. He put his hand on my shoulder, and I drifted off.

My dad was a handsome man, and when he smiled, people smiled back. He was an expert in the art of small talk, and he had a way of making people feel instantly at ease. When we climbed out of the Jeep at the Deer Park Elks Club the next morning, I watched him as we stood in line. "Boy, it's cold," he said. "Makes my nipples hard."

"Be careful," a large man said. "You don't want to get me excited."

A few guys laughed, and before I knew it we were all standing in a circle, joking around. There were a few boys there my age, and a cute girl who looked like she was in high school. She was tall, with shoulder-length brown hair and flushed cheeks. She rocked back and forth, shifting from foot to foot, occasionally blowing into her cupped hands and then rubbing them together. "Don't get outshot by her," my dad whispered. "Nothing worse than getting outgunned by a girl."

I kept quiet the whole morning. I didn't expect so many people, and so much chewing and spitting. After a while, an old, wiry man stood up on the bed of a pickup with a bullhorn in his hand.

"Welcome to the first annual Northwest White-Tailed Buck Shoot-Out. As you know, there are some pretty big cash prizes and some nice consolation gifts. For example, whoever brings in the buck with the strangest antlers, as judged by my wife, Marianne, and her three friends, Hazel, Vi, and Sharon . . ." The old guy pointed over to the front door of the Elk's Club. Four ladies were standing there in floral patterned jackets. They waved to us. ". . . will receive a free tune-up at my shop in Spokane."

Someone yelled, "What if you live in Montana?"

"Well," the old man said, "get it on the way out." He went on to explain the rules. We would have all weekend. The deadline for bringing in the kills would be set at 4 p.m. on Sunday afternoon. The official hunting territory began on the north side of Deer Lake and continued northward into the Kaniksu National Forest. "Just follow the signs, gentlemen. There's plenty of room for every-body." He went on to give us safety tips that everyone knew and then he said, "Now, last summer, there were a lot of fires up in that forest, and you all know what that means. It should be a good year. All the second-growth timber up there provides a nice feeding ground for the deer. It'll probably be like shooting kids in a candy store. But gentlemen, don't shoot everything in sight. Remember, we're only going after the bucks. Please leave the women and chil-dren alone." He then held a pistol up in the air and yelled, "Boy, howdy! Let's getta huntin'!" He pulled the trigger, and the gun blasted, sending echoes across the fields. The men started whoop-ing and hollering as they climbed into their trucks.

My dad pulled out a cigarette and said, "Well, what are you standing there for? We got some bucks to kill."

This was it. This was the pinnacle, the culmination of all my child-hood fantasies. This was like a kid who spends all of his time looking at the stars through a telescope, finally hopping on a space shuttle and going up there to look at Ursa Minor with his naked eye, taking pictures and, I'm sure, like me, shaking in his boots. What if I locked up? What if my finger refused to pull the trigger? All of this ran through my head as I climbed into the Jeep. What didn't cross my mind was the conspicuous absence of Dad's hunt-ing partners—Sheen, Dunkirk, Mayfield, Rodgers, Leone, and the others he'd mentioned in the past.

It had started to snow and the trail we hiked in on had a light dusting that displayed human footprints. The wind was at our back, sending our scent down the trail ahead of us. Dad assured me that when we got farther in we would find a fresh trail and embark on "our singular mission." He pulled out a cigarette and started smoking one after the other. We walked on for an hour or two or three and suddenly we were right back at the roadside. "Jesus," Dad said. "Would you look at our luck?" He shook his head and then hiked down to the Jeep.

"Where are you going?" I said.

"I don't know about you, but I'm freezing." He hopped into the Jeep and cranked it over. I stood on the hillside, snow landing softly on my shoulders, and I looked at him in the Jeep, rubbing his hands, blowing on them. The afternoon was creeping on, and I knew we were done for the day. I got into the Jeep and said, "That was fun."

"Hey, listen," he said, "we weren't going to get anything today anyway. You knew that. What's the first rule of the hunt?"

"Um, let's see, no smoking?"

"Real funny, Redd Foxx," he said. "Does the saying 'early bird gets the worm' mean anything to you? What do you say we go back to the motel, get some sleep and wake up real early? Tomorrow we can be miles in as the sun rises."

This would have been fine if all the other hunters weren't camping deep in the woods. I'd never even heard of hunters staying in motels. This one was called Eagle's Landing, and on top of the motel sign stood a sculpture that looked like an owl painted with black and white eagle markings. The walls in the motel room were covered with dark wood paneling. Light from the parking lot shone through the floral patterned curtains that wouldn't close all the way, and water dripped a constant trickle into a dirty bathtub.

Dad fell asleep with the TV on, and then woke up in the middle of the night to the high-pitched buzz and the Indian face. He got up and turned off the TV. When he got back in his bed, into the darkness he said, "I wonder why they picked an Indian."

The next morning we started hiking in the dark, and as the gray early-morning light spread its way through the snow-covered forest, Dad spotted some fresh scrapes on a Douglas fir. Bucks rub their antlers on trees to mark their territory, and this buck looked big because of the size of the tree.

"See this?" Dad said. "There's another one over there. Done last night. He moved right through here." He was much quieter now and he motioned for me to follow him.

"Dad," I whispered.

He stopped and looked back at me.

I grabbed the pheromones from my backpack.

"What are you doing?" he said.

"I'm going to spread this on the tree. It'll draw him here. It's doe scent."

"Walt, we have to go *to* the deer. It won't come to us."

I spread it on the tree and pulled out the deer rattle I had ordered from the back of Buck MacGuire's journal. "Dad, all we have to do is climb up a tree and rattle this for a while until the buck comes back."

"What are we, monkeys? Do I look like an ape to you?" he said. "Tell you what, partner, *you* climb the damn tree. If you want to freeze to death, go ahead. I'm going to hunt down this son-of-a-bitch and I'm going to kill him."

"But Dad, in all the books it says that when it gets cold they start to reproduce and they compete with other males, that's why the rattle works."

"You and all your damn books," he said. "What are you going to believe? Some ink on paper, or me? Huh? Now I'm heading down this trail."

I knew I couldn't stay alone in those woods, so I put the rattle back in my pack, and sauntered behind him. Maybe he was right, maybe the deer was just down the trail a ways, grazing or scraping his antlers on another tree. We inched along a narrow trail that looked as if it was created by animals. It didn't have that loose, sloppy feel of a manmade trail. It wasn't long before Dad found deer tracks, little heart-shaped prints in the snow.

We crouched down and spied through the bushes. He gave me his binoculars, and I panned all the way around us. There was nothing.

"Let's stay down and go along this trail awhile," he whispered. "Follow his tracks."

It looked like the buck was heading down to the lake. I told Dad this. He nodded, and we hunched low and strained our way down the trail. After a few minutes my thighs were burning and my heart was jumping all around my chest. I could feel something special, and I just knew we were getting close.

But as the day went on, the buck's tracks disappeared under the layers of falling snow, and soon our only concern was finding our way back to the Jeep. It was hard for me to admit failure. I wanted to keep hunting. But Dad convinced me that before too long it would be dark and we'd be stuck.

As we walked back, Dad told me stories, trying to cheer me up. "One time Murphy, and I'm not shitting you here, Murphy gut-shot this elk, and we had to chase that damned ugly thing for miles, until finally it runs out onto this ice-covered lake. Well, Murphy shoots it again, this time smack dab in the heart. So the thing stumbles around, and splat! It falls on the ice. And guess what happened? The ice breaks. No kidding, the ice breaks and it squeals or something, the ice, as it's breaking, this long squeal. One second that old, dumb elk was there, the next it was lying on the bottom of the lake."

We moved on and eventually Dad was silent, and I knew that we were lost. It was still snowing, and it was now beginning to get dark. Eventually Dad stopped and pulled out his flashlight and compass. We were due east of where we'd begun. "Well," he said, "go west, young man!"

"Westward ho!" I said.

He smiled at me and then turned and started moving quickly, which scared me. After a while it was pitch-black except for the beam of light scanning the trail in front of us.

"This was the trail we came in on, isn't it?" he said.

"I don't know."

"Jesus, I didn't know we'd hiked in so far," he said.

It had been dark a long while now, and the temperature had dropped. My toes and fingers were getting numb, and my nostrils were freezing shut.

Dad turned and put his arms around my shoulders. I fell into him. "Don't worry, Walt. It'll be okay. We'll be fine." He held me up. I was exhausted. "We're close," he said. "Let's just keep moving."

I fell behind again, and as I looked up at his back moving through the darkness, all the pieces began to fall into place, all of the holes in his charade became clear to me, and I began to list them under my breath.

"What was that?" he said. "What the hell did you say?"

"There was never any venison. You never brought home deer meat."

"What are you talking about?"

"You can always buy a deer head."

He stopped and pointed the flashlight in my face.

"You're not a hunter," I said. My whole body seized up. I looked down to get the light out of my eyes. "Are you?"

I didn't want to pursue it, because part of me, a large part, wanted him to be what he always was—a courageous woodsman, a man who knew how to get us back to the Jeep, to safety. I looked up into the small beam of the flashlight and said, "You can't even shoot straight."

He pointed the light down on the trail between us, and took a deep breath and said, "Yeah, well." And then he turned and started moving away from me. I wanted him to fight, to prove me wrong, counter my claims with evidence to convince me otherwise. I wanted him to offer up Dunkirk or Sheen, men who were there on past trips, witnesses to his hunting prowess. It was amazing how, faced with the truth, the truth that I myself had spoken, I still wanted to be told, and to believe, a lie.

When I caught up to him, he was pulling the flare gun out of his backpack. "I've hunted once or twice, Walt. But I've never killed anything." He said this with a nonchalance that betrayed everything I was feeling, as if it were a bit of news from the Sunday paper. He obviously didn't understand the impact it had on me. "But you're right, Perry Mason." He held up the flare gun and pulled the trigger. The ball of fire shot up and hit the branch of a tall pine tree with a loud smack. It ricocheted and spiraled down into the snow and fizzled out. But it had given us enough light to see that we were only a hundred feet or so from the road. When Dad saw this, his body changed, and before I knew it, we were both running to the end of the trail. The Jeep was just a ways down from where we'd come out of the woods, and as we climbed in, Dad turned on the heater and told me to take off my boots. "Get some circulation to your feet," he said.

I didn't find out the real story until years later. It turns out that whenever he went away on one of his hunting expeditions, he was really up in Vancouver seeing a woman named Anita Brice.

Of course I didn't know this at the time. All I cared about, as I sat in the Jeep, was getting feeling back into my fingers and toes. It was so dark that even with my adjusted eyes, my dad was hardly visible. "That was crazy, wasn't it?" he said, his voice filling the darkness.

He turned on the lights. The dashboard lit up and I could see his profile as he looked out the windshield. "How do your hands feel?"

"They hurt."

"That's good. That means you're getting some feeling back."

Dad pulled onto the highway. The road was dark and empty, and as the snow descended, I grew drowsy. I could feel myself giving in to the warmth, letting it cradle me, as my head eased down against the door.

Sometime later, I awoke to Dad swerving all over the icy road and sliding to a stop. "Holy crap," he said. He put the Jeep in reverse and drove back down the road and slid to a stop again. Then he brought the Jeep forward, the tires digging into the untouched snow on the side of the road. In the headlights before us lay a buck, his body jerking and kicking in the thick powder. Dad cut the engine and got out. The deer froze. I could hear snow crunching under Dad's feet. He stopped in front of the Jeep, his shoulders and head rising into the darkness above the headlights. It was quiet now, and still. Snow covered everything. Dad's door hung open, and the cold air pricked at my skin.

It took me this long to realize that Dad had hit the buck, that by some freak accident, after we'd unsuccessfully tracked deer all day, one had jumped out in front of us as we were driving back to the motel. Dad moved away from the deer, looked up and down the road, and then ran to the Jeep, and grabbed his rifle.

"Come on, boy!" he said. "We got ourselves a buck!"

It had to be a dream, I told myself. This couldn't be happening. My dad climbed onto the hood and pointed the rifle down at the deer. It was scraping its front legs on the snow. The shot blast went off, but the deer kept moving. Dad didn't hit it in the heart. He hit the chest, but too high up, too close to the spine. The deer kept breathing, blood splattered on the snow around him. Dad climbed down and looked in at me. "Are you gonna help me or what?"

I slipped on my boots and got out. Shadows moved around Dad's face as he stepped over the deer. "I'll get the torso, you grab the head."

He was an eight-point buck. His antlers were huge, making his head small by comparison. Dad put his arms around the buck's belly and I wrapped mine around his neck. His eyes were open, and he was looking at me. Breath shot out of his mouth in tiny puffs. He had stopped kicking. He was now waiting to die.

Dad crouched down and counted to three and we hoisted the deer onto the hood. Blood was everywhere. It covered my shoulder and arm, and it dripped down the Jeep's grille. A large patch of red snow was at our feet in the pool of headlights. Dad got the rope out and started tying the buck down. It was obvious he didn't know what he was doing. He wrapped every part of the buck's anatomy, until it was mess of rope and flesh.

When we got back to the motel, Dad was afraid to leave the buck on the hood of the Jeep all night, afraid someone might steal it. "It's a competition, Walt. There's money at stake."

I refused to help him, deciding instead to crawl under the covers.

"Suit yourself," he said.

A while later, the door flew open, and Dad staggered backward, trying to maneuver the buck's legs through the door. He dragged the deer in on a green canvas tarp and left him there, at the foot of my bed.

When I woke up in the morning, the smell of blood and deer musk filled the room. Dad was snoring. I could hear the cleaning lady vacuuming the room next door.

I got up and put on some clothes. The buck lay there watching me with his dead, blank stare. His mouth was hanging open, as if he'd died expecting something.

A little later, while Dad was out tying the buck down, I was in the motel room, scrubbing the blood that had soaked into the carpet. Dad's plan was to go to the Elks Club and claim that he'd shot the buck. He'd created an entire story in case anybody asked, and he wanted me to go along with it. But I was now so disillusioned, so thoroughly disgusted that, while I scrubbed, while the rag turned red in my hand, I came up with a different plan.

A gray pall covered the early afternoon sky. Snow no longer fell, but it was everywhere, packed onto the parking lot of the Elks Club, causing the men to slip and stagger as they untied the deer and carried him to an old rusted scale. I sat in the Jeep and watched as my dad approached the old man who was running the competition. Several men looked on as they hoisted the buck onto the scale. The girl was there, the teenage girl with her brown hair and flushed cheeks. She was standing by the scale in a red knit cap, looking at the dead deer.

I climbed out of the Jeep to a deep voice shouting, "Two hundred and twenty-three pounds!"

My dad was signing papers and bragging about the buck. I walked across the snow-packed parking lot, through the hoards of men who were murmuring about the biggest buck of the competition now slumped on the scale by my father.

"Sir?" I said. "Sir?"

"Yes?" the old man said. "What is it?"

My father smiled at me as if I was going to add detail to his story. The men around us looked on, waiting for me to say something. Breath shot out of my mouth in little gusty clouds.

"What is it you wanted to say, son?" my father said.

The man behind the table ran his hand over his beard.

I looked up at my father, who was now squinting down at me. "Walt," he said, his voice a kind of dog growl, "what do you have to say?"

I turned to the old man and, just as he was about to go back to the forms on the table and forget about me, I said, "Sir, he didn't shoot that deer."

"What?" my dad said. "What did you say?"

"You didn't shoot that deer."

It was suddenly silent. The girl looked at me, her eyebrows raised.

"What did you say, boy?" the old man said.

The faces of the men turned in my direction.

"I said, he didn't shoot that deer."

The old man turned to my father. "Is that true?"

My father peered up at all of the men looking at him, and then he turned and faced me. He let out a sigh and shook his head, a smile forming on his face. "It's true," he said. "It's true."

Everybody started to talk. And I immediately felt sorry for him.

My father took his eyes off me and looked around. "What can I say?" he said. "It wouldn't be fair to the boy for me to take credit for something he did."

It took a moment for everyone to comprehend the full meaning of what he'd said. But then everything happened so quickly, like a swift current taking me by the ankles and yanking me under. The men were suddenly shouting, all around me, loud voices, hands clapping. "How old are you, boy?" They circled around me and pushed me up to the table.

"Twelve!" my dad shouted. He was smiling, a proud father. To him it was a simple revision of the story, no less glorious—I was the son he had reared to be courageous in battle, as if I were genetic proof of his own indisputable bravery.

The voices grew louder at the mention of my age. The girl smiled at me. She was so pretty right then, I swear it hurt to even look at her. A pen was placed in my hand. The old man put his finger where it said signature. And for some reason I couldn't say anything, I couldn't stop any of it. As my hand moved across the paper, I saw my name scribbled out—Walter Berry—and I suddenly thought that the name was not mine, that it was a creation, a character formed in my imagination, a character in a story in *Buck MacGuire's Big Game Journal.*

I was going to be a celebrity, they said. My picture in *Field and Stream*, write-ups in various papers. The youngest person to ever win a major hunting competition. They started taking pictures of me posed beside the deer. Some guy from the *Spokesman Review* told me to smile and relax. "Don't look so shocked!" The flash popped. "One more," he said.

My dad stood back, in the distance, smiling at me. It happened so quickly, the truth never came out. What can you say with all that excitement around you? If you do say anything, don't you spoil their fun, their desire to hope, to believe that the impossible is possible? But now I had learned of the irrevocable nature of stories, how they turn necessarily by their own design, formed by circumstance and longing.

As it turned out, someone came in later that day with a bigger buck, and I got second place and a prize of five hundred dollars cash. The same two men who untied the deer tied him back onto the Jeep with a precision that I'm sure embarrassed my father.

After the awards ceremony in the Elks Lodge, Dad and I pulled out onto Highway 2. We drove through the frozen farmland of eastern Washington in silence. I occasionally glanced over at him, but he was concentrating only on the road in front of us. He didn't look at me or say anything for hours, and I knew that he'd no longer be telling me his hunting stories, and I'd have to get used to this silence, and eventually we'd have to learn to talk about other things. But as we headed into the apple orchards of the Columbia River Basin, as we passed over the swirling blue water, I started concocting my own stories—of how I spotted the buck in a clearing hundreds of yards away, how my rattle brought him to me, and how I looked down the barrel of my gun and calmly pulled the trigger—stories I would tell my friends at school the next day, my teachers, my mom, anyone who would listen.

Free Spirits

I've been waiting for the voices, for the incoherence of psychosis, for evidence, substantiation, other than my crooked teeth and lazy eye, that I am indeed my father's son. I've been anticipating, turning my head in alarm when a dry leaf scratches along the sidewalk, as if a whisper has found its way into my head. But the voices have never come.

It's absurd, I know, but part of me wanted them to arrive, wanted the fits of mania, the sleepless nights. But the other day, as I walked through the doors of the facility he lives in, I was thankful that I had never experienced his illness. Whenever I visit him I'm filled with a queer sense of sadness and gratitude. This is how I felt when I wandered into the community room and saw my father slumped over a table.

Harold and Mitch were playing Ping-Pong and beyond them, Claire and Darlene were staring at a TV, its picture struggling through static. "Hello, Arthur," Mitch said to me in that belabored way of his. "Did you bring me some Gummi Bears?"

"Sorry, Mitch. No Bears today." I looked down at my father who now stared into the kitchen. "Hey, Pop. What's shaking?"

"Somebody stole my socks," he said. "A new pair. A new pair of socks."

Karen, his case manager, a tall, gangly graduate student with a pronounced, but not unattractive, overbite, came out of the office and touched his shoulder. He pulled away from her and looked at the floor.

"We'll get you a new pair," she said, pushing her straight blond hair behind her left ear. She walked into the kitchen, her khakis hanging loosely from her narrow hips. She put something into the microwave, and then looked at me and smiled. "How are you, Arthur?" she asked. "You didn't bring any flowers today."

My father knew things. Growing up, I thought he knew everything. And in a way he did. He was an information specialist for an encyclopedia company that was responsible for most of the knocking on suburban doors at dinnertime, for the aching shoulders of the door-to-door salesmen, for all the plagiarism exacted by third graders reporting on Bolivia or the habitat of the gila monster. My father was tireless with knowledge, and he drilled my brother, Samuel, and me with the zeal of a charismatic. By the age of seven I knew all the capitals of the world. By eight I could discourse at length on the tools of the Mesolithic Age.

I remember a Sunday trip to Catalina Island, and strangers gathered at the bow of the boat to watch Samuel and me in amazement.

"The colloidal substance constituting the living matter in plants and animals," my father said, pointing to Samuel.

The crowd peered down at my little brother, who stood there, grinning, as if to say, *It's going to take more than that to stump me.*

"Protoplasm," he said.

Everybody laughed and applauded for the little genius in the Dodger cap.

My father, raising the ghost of P.T. Barnum, cleared his throat and clapped his hands. "The first period of the Cenozoic Era—Arthur?"

Over my father's shoulder I saw a seagull gliding through the pale blue sky, and behind and below me the Pacific folded over on itself and pushed away from the boat in white, billowing swells. Even as a nine-year-old I knew this exercise was a waste of time. I knew that information and knowledge couldn't make you happy. My father's head was full of data, yet he was the saddest person I knew. He'd started to lose control and had begun taking medication after eight sleepless nights and an encounter with police officers outside the public library, where he'd been hurling books into traffic.

"What's the point if it makes you miserable?" my mother had said—my mother who believed in astrology and the philosophy of Ann Landers. And I understood that while my father knew the facts, my mother probably knew the truth.

But standing on a boat halfway between San Pedro and Avalon, with the wind at my back and the tourists looking at me as if I were the three-eyed wonder boy with webbed feet and a penchant for belching the "Star-Spangled Banner," I felt overcome by a Pavlovian pull to answer my father.

"Arthur?" he said, trying to draw it out of me.

I took a deep breath. "Tertiary," I said.

. . .

Now, Karen, for some reason, has always flirted with me. I don't know why. Not only does she know everything about my father's illness—and thus the potential calamity of my own genetic makeup—but she also knows about my abnormal childhood. And believe me on this, I am no piece of art. I have narrow shoulders, unmanageable moppy brown hair, and a complexion that is insub-ordinate at best. But every time I come to visit my father, Karen gives me these looks that are uncommon for me, and thus make me rather uncomfortable. "Is there a place I can talk with my father alone?" I asked her.

"Oh, sure," she said. "You can use my office."

Oak Crest is a facility that serves the homeless mentally ill. My father has been living here for almost a year. He is on probation for destroying hundreds of library books, and for him Oak Crest serves as a kind of alternative sentencing program. His diagnosis is 296.6X, Bipolar Disorder, Mixed, with psychotic features, which means he has manic cycles, where he goes days without sleep and becomes irritable and arrogant and starts hearing voices—God, or Noah Webster, or Stephen Hawking—and then cycles down into a deep depression. When he takes his meds his behavior stabilizes, and he is pleasant, but apathetic. He has never consistently taken his meds, however, as his pride has blinded him to his illness.

For the last twenty years he has bounced in and out of such facilities, and with a few exceptions they are all the same—speckled tiled floors, long hallways, fluorescent lights; a large room with a Ping-Pong table, or a pool table, or both, and a TV that rarely works; young, eager grad students just starting on their master's in social work, and caregivers who roll their eyes, smoke cigarettes, and tell jokes about the clients.

Karen let us into her office, chatting with me about how good my father had been lately. "He even asked to help clean the dishes yesterday," she said.

Two desks sat on opposite sides of the cluttered mauve room. An old black file cabinet leaned against the wall. Karen cleared a few things off her desk and pulled the chair out for me.

"He's really coming along here." She leaned toward me and whispered, "I think your visits are good for him."

"Well, that's nice to hear."

"We always look forward to family visits," she said. "Isn't that right, William?"

My father sat on a plastic chair in the middle of the office staring at me. "Do you have my cigarettes?" he asked.

"Well, I'll see you later," Karen said, and closed the door behind her.

"Yes," I told him. "I brought the cigarettes and the latest issue of *Parabola*. There's an article I thought you'd like about Icelandic mythology."

"How's Samuel?" my father asked.

Samuel didn't mind the gawking strangers. He seemed amused by all the attention, and he handled it with the insouciance of a wily old stage actor. I, on the other hand, soon began to despise my father for his insistence, his absolute need to fill my brain with minutiae and then show off my "supposed" intellect to the world. And so I avoided him whenever I could by spending afternoons in my mother's garden.

My mother never seemed to care about all the small facts fighting for space in my brain. She never quizzed me on the history of crossbreeding, or the unique blooming characteristics of the yellow evening primrose. She went about her work in the haphazard fashion of someone in love. She would pop up on the other side of the birds-of-paradise and catch her breath. "Look at this," she'd say, holding a bulb in the air. "It's like a little potato." She'd wipe the sweat from her forehead with the back of her hand. "But then it becomes a flower."

My mother met my father on the night after Nixon's 1962 concession speech. She was at Margie Dube's house listening to Kingston Trio records when Margie's brother started laughing hysterically down the hall. Margie and my mother went to see what was so funny. Apparently my father, at eighteen, was pulling an impressive Nixon impersonation. And when Nixon made the remark, "you won't have Dick Nixon to kick around anymore," my father said "you won't kick my dick around anymore."

My mother, shocked by this, let out a shriek of laughter, and the more she laughed the more my father laid it on, shaking his jowls and blurting out expletives. By the end of the night, he was smitten. But he kept his feelings secret for weeks, until one evening when he summoned up enough courage to appear unannounced at my mother's doorstep with a bouquet of yellow roses.

My mother's mother opened the door, and my father said, "Forgive me, Mrs. Hoff, for being forward by appearing at your house without prior engagement, but I can assure you my rudeness is exceeded only by the fondness I have for your daughter."

They dated on and off for nearly three years, and then one night my mother, who was nineteen years old, stumbled into the bathroom and leaned over the porcelain bowl, praying for sickness, for food poisoning, for something other than a sperm joined with an egg. But there I was, lodged in a body that didn't want me, that rode beside my father down Highway 101 toward my premature and necessary end.

I often think about what would have happened had my father not turned off impetuously toward the ocean, if he'd kept going south to Tijuana, where such procedures were common and cheap. What would have happened if my father hadn't jumped out of the car, and pulled my mother toward the dark, falling Pacific, if he hadn't gotten romantic and sentimental, saying that the world is full of purpose, that the waves tumble as they are supposed to, that the sky holds the promise of reason in its celestial light?

When my mother tells this story, I find it impossible to picture my father on the beach with her. In my mind there's a shadowy figure silhouetted by the moon, but it's not my father. I have always felt betrayed by this dichotomy, the man she talks about has never been the man I know.

Living with my father was like living in the tundra: when his sun was at its brightest it shone for days on end, and when darkness fell we couldn't expect to see light for a long time. For a while, my father contained himself enough to hold on to his job. But around the house, his changes became drastic and frighteningly unpredictable. So my mother and I would escape him by working in her garden.

The entire southeast corner of our backyard was filled with flowers. She called it her English garden, which I took to mean a garden without discrimination, a wild garden, displaying all the mayhem of longing she found perhaps only in her dreams, or lying awake at night in that distinct darkness of regret. I helped her plant some of those flowers. My fingers pressed the dirt around the roots of the bleeding hearts and the begonias, and I helped her pick out the fuchsias and the primroses. But my favorite flower of all was the shooting star, an odd, rare wildflower my mother and I found rising out of dry, hard earth on the side of the Angeles Crest Highway one Sunday afternoon. Its stem was thin and spindly, and it rose nearly two feet high with sharp, lavender petals springing out in all directions. My mother put the shovel under it, and we took it home and planted it by a pink daffodil. To our surprise, it survived, and lived through the winter, showing its petals again the first week of April.

My father took exception to my interest in gardening, as if I were betraying his trust in some way. A few days before my tenth birthday he cornered me in the utility room, the washing machine shaking at my back. "Tell me," he said. "I know you know it, goddammit!" He was whispering so my mother, who was outside waiting for me, would not hear him.

"I don't know and I don't care!" I said.

He had asked me in which direction the Panama Canal flowed, and then threatened to make me conjugate Latin verbs all night until I came up with the answer.

"What the hell's the matter with you?" he asked. His face was sallow, and his skin drooped around his eyes.

The sliding glass door rattled on its rails. "Arthur?" my mother said. "Are you coming outside?"

My father turned and let me move by him. "Fine," he whispered. "Get out."

"Sam is doing fine," I said.

My father fingered his beard, which looked like a bird's nest glued to his face. He let out a strange, staggered huff, and said, "Samuel was always perfunctory."

"How do you mean?"

"I didn't lose my socks," he said.

He could always dissociate like this, swerving from thought to thought.

"You didn't say you lost them. You said somebody stole them."

"Nobody stole my socks," he said. "It keeps things interesting." He was now circling his hands around his kneecaps. "Sam is okay? How is that wife of his?"

"Sheila's doing fine, Dad," I said. "She left him, you know."

"Why?"

"I don't know. Maybe it was that affair he was having with that paraseismologist at Cal Tech." I hadn't spoken to my little brother in more than six months, and had in that time become a companion of sorts to his wife. I found myself, much to my surprise, thinking about her quite a lot lately. Phone calls after midnight were now fairly common. "What the hell is wrong with your brother?" she'd say.

What could I tell her that wouldn't in some way taint her image of me too?

"These people around here," my father said. "If I keep on them, they'll be looking for those socks for days."

Sitting in that decaying office, trying to sustain a conversation with my father, I was suddenly disheartened. "Dad, do you want to go for a ride?"

"I need new glasses," he said.

"Come on. Let's get out of here." I stood up and, against my better judgment, started for the door on the opposite side of the room. "Let's get some fresh air." I knew, even as I unlocked the door and quietly eased it open, that he could get into trouble for this.

"Almost robotic," he said. "Had no kick in him. A bit of a sycophant if you ask me." I knew my father well enough to know that he was referring to my brother, Sam, and that "perfunctory nature" of his. "You weren't like that," he said. "Remember, it's the fighters who are respected, martyrs are merely worshipped, and worshippers ridiculed."

For my tenth birthday my mother gave me a piece of the backyard between the myrtle and the juniper, and told me I could do whatever I wanted with it. So I dug up the sod and prepared my plot of land. While my father locked himself in his room, my mother took Sam and me to Imperial Gardens Nursery in South Pasadena and told me to get what I needed. I picked two heliotropes, two gardenias, a sweet alyssum, several peonies, Hall's honeysuckle for ground cover, a daphne shrub for a centerpiece, a star jasmine, a poet's jasmine, a true jasmine, and four night jasmine.

As I carried the flowers into the backyard, I saw my father through the screen door in the kitchen. He was in his white boxer shorts, talking on the phone. "I'll be in Monday, Jack." I set the crate of flowers on the ground and heard him shout, "Please, Jack? I said I'll be in Monday! I'll be there."

It was the last week of July, and as I dug, the topsoil crumbled into dusty granules. I put the hose on it for a few minutes and then resumed digging. The first to go in was the daphne with its curling clusters of pink and white petals, and then the various jasmines.

Before long I had forgotten about my father's pleading, his almost naked body outlined in the shaded kitchen window. I was in my garden, planting my flowers, and as I finished, placing the honeysuckle around the heliotrope and gardenia, I was struck by the strange feeling of joy, which was so rare that I didn't recognize it as joy, but as a queer sense of unbalance and displacement.

After I'd been sitting beside my garden a while, the hose now turned off but still dangling from my hand, my mother came out of the house and stopped midway through the yard. "It's beautiful, Arthur," she said.

"You should come closer and smell it."

My mother stood there in the evening sun looking at the garden but not really focused on anything. Her head dropped down, and she brought her right hand up and pinched the bridge of her nose. Her left hand moved around her rib cage, feebly hugging her torso, which had started rising and falling with each gasp. Unable to say anything, I looked away, thinking maybe she would stop soon and talk about my garden. But she continued, quietly struggling to inhale, and as I listened, a disgust rose inside me, a bitterness at what her tears were confirming, what we'd been so good at avoiding for so long.

She looked up and took her hands away from her eyes. "Arthur," she said, "this garden is wonderful." She composed herself and inched closer. "You must be so proud of it."

"It doesn't really smell that good yet," I said.

The sliding glass door flew open and sent a shuddering boom across the backyard. "This is where you went?" my father shouted. He came out onto the patio and paced back and forth. "This is where?" he said. "This is where?" He clenched his fists, shook out his fingers, and then clenched his fists again.

It was usually about this time that my mother would put Sam and me in the Plymouth and head over to the Denny's in Eagle Rock, where we'd sip milkshakes and listen to the chatter of people in other booths. But he was escalating quickly and I could see the decision clearly in my mother's eyes. This evening we weren't going anywhere.

. . .

As my father and I ducked out of Oak Crest, the Santa Ana winds whipped the palm trees. Leaves and debris swirled through the parking lot. My father, oblivious to the elements, climbed into the car. The mood stabilizers he was on were a little too effective, making his facial expressions as blunt as a mallet. He stared out the windshield as if he did this every day.

I drove through the dusty streets of Pacoima and found my way to the 210, which on this Sunday afternoon was virtually empty. The wind, surging through the mountain passes, pushed my little Subaru all over the road.

My father chewed on his chapped bottom lip and looked out the window at the dry boulders and sagebrush of the Big Tujunga wash. "How's your mother?" he asked.

"She's doing fine," I said.

"Yeah?" he said. "And that husband?"

"How did you know about Richard?"

"She called me. We talked."

My mother had remarried recently, and in an attempt to be considerate I withheld the news of her marriage from my father.

"How come you didn't tell me?" he said.

"It never came up."

"Dr. Spencer told me to let go," he said.

"Let go of what?"

"Where are we going?" he said. "I don't feel too good about this."

"Don't worry about it. You won't get into trouble. I'll tell them I kidnapped you."

"She said she was happy," he said. "Might be moving down to

San Diego with Richard after she retires." A smirk crossed his face. "So, he's a mailman, huh?"

"A postmaster," I said. "He runs the post office."

"I know what a postmaster is," he said. "She said she might come out and see me. How's she look?"

I glanced at my father, who looked old and worn. And then I thought of my mother who was still an attractive woman. "She's about the same, I guess."

"I have to get some new clothes for when she comes out."

"That's a good idea," I said, peeking down at his fuzzy green cardigan, bulging over a white LA Rams sweatshirt.

"Dr. Spencer makes sense. Years with these people and finally a man, a Princeton man at that, who isn't full of shit."

"What did he tell you to let go of?"

"Everything," he said, looking out the window. "And nothing."

We skirted through the Verdugo Mountains, the brown humps of the San Gabriels on our port side, past La Tuna Canyon and a small par-three golf course rimmed with rhododendrons.

He cleared his throat and said, "So when are you going to get married?"

I laughed and shook my head.

"You like being alone?" he said.

"What are you talking about?" I said. "I stay busy." I gripped the wheel as a strong gust pushed us toward the right lane. "I mean, sometimes, you know, it would be nice, I guess, to have someone." Just then, I thought about Sam's soon-to-be ex, Sheila, about her small mouth and her big laugh, and how lately I lay in bed hoping for the phone to ring.

"What wonder that we free spirits are not exactly the most communicative spirits?" my father said.

"What?"

"That we do not wish to betray in every respect what a spirit can free itself from."

"Where'd you get that?" I said.

My father yawned and leaned his head back. "I've been going through the existentialists again."

"Hm. Sartre?"

"Nietzsche," he said, disgusted. "Sartre was a coward!"

I didn't know what to say. The halting and awkward nature of our previous discussions, which I'd grown used to, was now gone, and we were having a somewhat normal conversation, which made me uncomfortable.

I pulled off the 210 and headed into Pasadena's suburban, Spanish-flavored neighborhoods. I'd forgotten how close our old house was to the freeway. Within a few moments we were parked in front of the house I was raised in.

My father peered down the street. "What are we doing here?" he asked.

"This is where?" my father repeated, pacing and clenching his fists. "This is where?"

"Can't this wait?" my mother said. "Please? It's Arthur's birthday." She turned to me and said, "Honey, why don't you go inside?"

But it was too late. My father rushed toward us. "This is where?" he shouted. "To your fucking garden?"

He picked up the shovel and started digging, the blade cutting into the peonies and honeysuckle. My mother lunged at him and grabbed his left arm. He turned and jammed his open palm into my mother's face with a loud smack, sending her backward, slumping onto the lawn. I threw my arms around him and tried to rip him down. His elbow smashed into my nose and I fell onto the ground, a sharp pain behind my eyes. When I looked up, he was standing over me with the shovel raised in the air. My mother screamed his name, and he looked down at me, his eyes like two unnamed stars, so distant, so far away from anything previously known, his face as blank as a dark shred of sky.

He was utterly confused, his eyebrows pushed down, his mouth open. My mother got up and took the shovel from his hands. His eyes hopped around in their sockets, and as my mother tried to touch him, he backed away, his head shaking uncontrollably. He turned and pushed the gate open and ran down the street. The sun was setting, and as the pink light of dusk filled our backyard on my tenth birthday, my father was running around our neighborhood in his boxer shorts.

While I held my head back with a bloody rag to my nose, my mother dialed 911. Sam, holding an odd Lego formation, came out of his room. "What's going on?" he said.

"Hello?" my mother said into the phone, her bottom lip swelling as she spoke. She gave information that was painful to hear, information that would lock my father up for a long time.

A few months later, after my mother had filed for divorce, we sold the house and moved into a duplex in Burbank. I didn't see my father again for three years.

The house was now beige (as opposed to the gray I remembered), with new stonework around its base, and a good-size addition where my bedroom used to be.

"Come on," I said, getting out of the car. I made my way to

the gate at the side of the house (the same gate he ran through thirty-one years before) and waited for him to climb out of the car. He was only sixty-five, but he moved like a much older man. He shuffled up beside me and said, "I don't think we should be here."

"Let's just look around," I said. I opened the gate and wandered into the backyard.

Very little had changed. There were bird feeders and birdhouses swaying from several trees that moved in the wind. And the trees had grown, filling up more of the yard. But other than that it looked much the same. My mother's garden was still there, but now it was full of malnourished roses, with faded petals. My little garden had been made bigger and was now being used to grow vegetables.

My father wandered over to the arbor, which still supported the wisteria, its vines whipping around slats of dried cedar. I knelt down at my old garden and scooped up a handful of soil. It was as dry and fine as I remembered, sliding easily through my fingers.

"I'm going back to the car," my father said.

His voice startled me. He was standing behind me, looking up at the myrtle, which was letting leaves go by the hundreds—thin, dry leaves raining down around us.

"North and south, Dad" I said. "Actually southeast to northwest. If you are coming from the west."

"Excuse me?"

"The direction of the Panama Canal," I said. "When you enter it from the west you are actually more east than when you exit."

"So?" he said.

"So you asked me once and I didn't answer," I said.

"You were stubborn," he said. "Big news."

"Why'd you have to ask me that? I mean, why was it so important to you?"

"You can't assume the direction of anything," he said. "From Limón Bay to Gatun Lake the canal goes due south and then turns eastward." He was suddenly his old self, offering information as if it held some deep significance. His face lit up as he held up his index finger and said, "But can you tell me precisely how long the canal is?"

"Funny," I said. "That's really funny."

"You don't know the answer," he said.

I turned back to my garden, fingering the dry remnants of a celery stalk. A long, looping siren wailed in the distance.

"That's why you don't respond," he said. "You don't know the answer."

"What?"

"Eighty-two kilometers. You didn't know that."

I stood up and faced him. "You know, Dad, I don't care about the length of the Panama Canal, or the circumference of Jupiter, for that matter, or Aristotle's rejection of the atomic theory."

"You don't care because you're ignorant. Knowledge forces you to care."

More sirens howled, and fire trucks rumbled down nearby streets as a fire somewhere scorched a hillside, the wind pushing the flames from shrub to shrub, or maybe it was a house, burning to the ground.

"You know what?" I said. "You can ask all the trivia questions you want, but I'm not going to answer them. I may be stupid or whatever, ignorant, I don't even care anymore. But I didn't come here to do this." I turned away from him and looked down at the parched soil in what used to be my garden. "I don't even know why I came." A row of wilting kale ran along the fence, and in front of that, anemic leaves rose up from the yellowing tops of Nantes carrots. "But it's good to see my garden, even if it's only vegetables."

"What garden?" he said. "You never had a garden."

"What did you say?"

"What garden?"

"My garden," I said. "Right here. For my birthday. Mom let me plant some flowers."

He looked at me, dumbfounded. "There was never a garden here."

"Excuse me?"

"I think we should go."

"You started digging everything I'd planted. And Mom was just trying to stop you. And you hit her. Right here," I said. "And then you hit me."

"What?" He stood there, his feet close together, one shoe untied, his sweatshirt frayed at the cuff. "I hit your mother?" The wind blew the hair around on his head. He looked up at me, as if searching for something to say. His eyes moved around, and I could tell he was trying to remember that day, trying to assemble the pieces of his life.

"Listen," I said. But I didn't know what else to say. The sirens had faded away, and the wind kicked up and died down, and for a moment it was quiet.

"You were young then," he said. "That was a long time ago."

"Excuse me?" I heard a voice say behind me. An old woman was standing on the other side of the screen door in the kitchen. "You're going to have to leave."

"Hello," I said. "I'm sorry. This is strange, I know, but we used to live here."

"Well, we'd appreciate it if you'd go now."

"Okay," I said. "We were just looking around, but we're leaving."

"Wait a minute," the lady said, staring at my father. She was like a ghost hovering behind the screen. "I thought I told you never to come back here. I told you I'd call the police if you ever came back."

"What?" I said.

My father turned away from me and walked across the lawn with the same nonchalance he'd have walking down the aisle of a supermarket, as if nothing had ever happened here. He pushed through the gate and disappeared as it slammed shut behind him.

"I'm calling the police," the lady said.

I stood in the middle of the yard. She could call the police. She could do whatever she wanted, but I wasn't going to leave, not yet.

I heard the car door creak open as my father got in, and then the faint sound of its closing. The woman behind the screen door was still looking at me. I didn't care. This at one time had been my backyard, this little piece of land, where my mother taught me about beauty and my father taught me about fear. Standing here, with the wind swirling around me, I took my time. I wasn't going to waste it.

The sliding glass door slammed shut and I heard the clicking of the lock. The woman disappeared behind the glass. I closed my eyes and listened to the wind, thankful that the voices had remained silent throughout my life that the wind sounded only like wind.

When I got back to the car, I pulled the keys from my pocket and climbed in. "Why didn't you tell me you'd been back here?" I said.

My father shrugged. I looked at the house and wondered why I hadn't come back before now, just a short drive across town. "What did you do to that woman?"

"Nothing," he said.

"You must have done something." I put the key in the ignition and started the car. "She threatened to call the police."

"I knocked on the door," he mumbled.

"Why?" I said. I put the car in gear and pulled out onto the road. "I don't get it."

"I don't know," he said. He leaned back and closed his eyes. "I was happy once."

I slowed to a stop at a red light, and when it turned green cars behind me started honking.

The Gypsy

Kupzyk sits in his run-down Chevette and waits for the inevitable. He leaves the key in the ignition and lets it idle, hoping that this will be quick. The engine sputters, returns to a low hum, then sputters again. Raindrops crawl down the fogged-up windshield and bounce on the car's gray hood.

There's a knock on the window. Kupzyk rolls it down and looks up at a young police officer, roughly Kupzyk's age, who stands under a large, black umbrella.

The officer scans the inside of the car, and then turns his gaze onto Kupzyk. "License, please."

Kupzyk hands the officer his license and says, "I'm sorry about that, back there, but I'm running a little late, and . . . ya' know . . ."

The officer examines Kupzyk's license. He turns it over, and then turns it over again, pursing his lips. "Well, Mr. Koopsack," he says, "do you know what stop signs are for?"

"Yes I do, and I'm sorry about that . . ."

"They're designed to stop cars."

"I know, and I'm really sorry."

"Mr. Koopsack," the cop says. "Do you mind if I ask you a personal question? Where you headin' in that getup?"

Kupzyk looks down his furry body to his feet covered with dark hair and latex toes. On the seat beside him a gorilla mask tilts back, scowling up at balloons that bob along the inside of the car.

"I'm kind of in a hurry actually," Kupzyk says. "You know, a performance thing. At the Holiday Inn."

"I see."

A small, graying officer walks up and looks into the car. "Well, what do we got here?" Raindrops spill off the bill of his navy blue cap.

"Look," Kupzyk says, "I'm truly sorry, but I'm running late and well, that's probably why I missed that stop sign and . . ."

"Guess where he's going?" the young cop says. "The Holiday Inn."

"Is that right?" the older officer says, peering down at Kupzyk. "In a monkey costume?"

"It's for a retirement party," Kupzyk says.

"Oh," the older cop says. "A singing telegram kind of thing."

"So, you going to sing a song in that get-up?" the young cop says, smiling at the older one. "A little dance number?"

They burst into laughter. The young officer shakes his head and says, "Woo," in a high-pitched voice. "A singing gorilla. Who thinks of these things?

"I'm sorry," Kupzyk says. "But I'm really in a hurry here."

The old cop straightens up and says, "Sergeant, isn't there a law explicitly stating that here in Iowa, monkeys have to drive by the same set of rules as humans?"

"Yes, sir."

"And are you aware of the many outstanding tickets this primate has stockpiled in the last six months?"

"No, sir."

"Well, he's going to have to do a lot of singing to pay for 'em. That's for sure."

The young cop squints into the car. "What song you going to sing today, Mr. Koopsack?"

"I'm not going to sing any song if I'm late."

"Well," the old cop says, "you can sing it for us then. What's it called?"

"What?"

"The name of the song, Mr. Koopsack."

Kupzyk stares straight ahead at the furry fingers that grip the steering wheel. He imagines his foot pushing down on the gas pedal, the wheels spitting gravel at the police car behind him.

"Mr. Koopsack?"

Kupzyk takes a deep breath and shakes his head. " 'Gypsy in My Soul.' "

"I don't think I've heard of that one," the young cop says.

The old cop says, "Sure you have. It's a classic."

"Look," Kupzyk says, "I'm running late here."

One hundred and five dollars, that's what he will lose if he doesn't get there in the next few minutes. One hundred and five dollars. Enough money for a couple bills and dinner tonight, Enough money to keep afloat for a few more days.

The old cop blinks at him. "Well, I'm sorry Mr. Koopsack, but I'm gonna have to ask you to step out of the car."

Kupzyk clenches his jaw and puts his head in his hands. "Please," he says. "Can you just give me a warning? I really have to get there, now!"

"I've got a Taser, Mr. Koopsask." The young cop says, placing his hand on his holster. "And I will use it."

"Fine!" Kupzyk cuts the engine and climbs out. A truck drives past, its tires sloshing along the wet pavement.

"Why don't you sing a little bit of that song?" the old one says, "so my partner can hear it."

Rain pelts Kupzyk's scalp and trickles down the sides of his head. The old cop crawls into the car and starts snooping around.

"Okay, let's hear it," the young cop says, dry under his umbrella.

"Jesus," Kupzyk says. He glances up the road, and thinks about running away. What's the cop going to do, shoot a guy in a gorilla suit?

"Are you going to sing or what?" the cop asks.

"Please," Kupzyk says. "I'd really appreciate it if we could just speed this up."

"You call that singing?"

Kupzyk takes in a long breath and closes his mouth. Several cars slow down as they pass, faces peering through rain-splattered windows.

"Hey, Jerry!" the young cop says. "The monkey don't wanna sing. What should we do to him?"

"Fine," Kupzyk says. He straightens up and opens his mouth. "No cares," he sings. "No strings. My heart has wings."

The old cop climbs out of the car with crumpled parking tickets in his balled-up fists.

"Well, well, well," the young cop says.

"So do you recognize it?" the old cop says. "The song?"

"Nope," the young one says. "Never heard it before. He's got a good voice, though. You hear that?"

"Come here," the old one says. "All that crap you listen to." He leads the young cop back to the police car. After they share a few words, the young cop slides into the driver's seat and gets on the phone.

Kupzyk climbs behind the wheel of the Chevette and turns the key in the ignition. The engine sputters.

"Hey! Mr. Koopsack!" the old cop says, running up to the side of the car. "Where you going?"

"I don't want to be arrested," Kupzyk says. "I'm making my getaway."

"What?" the cop says. "No one's arresting you. We're impounding your car. Now shut it off, Mr. Koopsack."

Kupzyk releases the key. The car mumbles and then is silent.

"Good," the cop says. "Might as well grab everything you need. The tow truck'll be here in a few."

Kupzyk runs a furry hand through his moppy brown hair, grabs the balloons, the mask, and the wallet, and climbs out of the car.

"Looks like about two hundred dollars for the parking tickets," the old cop says, "and another forty-five for running that stop sign. When you pay them off, you can come down to the yard and pick up your car."

Kupzyk pulls the mask down over his face. "Thank you officer," he says, his voice flat under the latex. "For everything, really." He reaches out his hairy paw and the cop grabs it.

"Break a leg today," the old man says. "That's one of my favorite songs."

Kupzyk sprints along the interstate, picking up his knees to avoid tripping over his feet. The balloons bob and jiggle behind him in the wind. The hotel is only a mile away, and if he hurries he can still get there in time to perform. He picks up his pace, sprinting, heaving his body along the brush that lines the road. Cars honk as they pass. Others slow down with their windows open, people leaning out and yelling things like, "Hey, monkey boy!" and "Look at that ape go!"

When he gets to the hotel, the wet balloons sag beside him, thunking into one another as he goes through the front doors and into the lobby. He rushes up to the front desk, his warm breath nearly choking him inside the mask. "Hi," he says. "I'm here for the party. The retirement party."

The lady behind the desk looks up from her computer and smiles at him, a smudge of maroon lipstick on her front teeth. "Well, hello. They've been waiting for you. I think they're all through, though. Should I put in a call?"

"No," Kupzyk says. "Please, just tell me where it is."

"Oh, well, you go down the hall there past the restrooms and the vending machines, they'll be on your right, and next to them is the ice machine and a drinking fountain, and just past that, well, you take a left and then you go down a ways and turn to your right and just down there . . ."

"Thank you." Kupzyk turns and sprints down the hallway. A white uniform flashes through the eyeholes of his mask as he runs into a maid walking out of the bathroom. "I'm sorry," he says. "Excuse me." He continues past the vending machines and the drinking fountain, and rushes to the left and then the right, where, down at the end of the hallway, a few people are smoking by an open door that leads out to the parking lot. Kupzyk hurries by them, into the banquet room, where dirty dishes are stacked on empty tables. Several people stand around, mingling.

"And this happened in Vermont!" someone says. And then laughter.

Heads turn in Kupzyk's direction, as he scans the room through the eyeholes of his mask, looking for Karen, the owner of Balloons & Tunes. He was supposed to meet her in the lobby a half-hour ago. That's how it works. He meets her beforehand, she watches the show and hands him a check. But she's nowhere in sight.

Kupzyk spots a microphone on a stand in the front of the room. He makes his way through the maze of messy tables and grabs the mike. "Hello?" he says. His voice leaps out and bounces around. "Is Don here?" He lays it on thick, like a clown, his voice animated and silly. "Oh, Donnie boy?" Over by the door an excited crowd gathers and pushes a stooped, old man toward him.

"You're not Don, are you? Well, you're much more handsome than they said you are. How many years has it been, Don?"

The old man mumbles something.

"What was that?"

"Fifty!" people shout.

"Fifty?" Kupzyk says. "Fifty years with one company." He pauses and thinks about that. The idea of spending so much time, an entire life in one place—driving to work every morning on the same roads, seeing the same people year after year—fills Kupzyk simultaneously with revulsion and respect. He looks closely at the old man in front of him. The way his skin droops off his bones reaffirms to Kupzyk the incredible force of gravity.

"Well, for that," Kupzyk says, "for all those years of service to Procter and Gamble, I have something for you." He moves over to Don and hands him the balloons. Don pushes out a chuckle and holds the balloons away from his body so they won't drip on him.

Kupzyk goes back to the microphone. "After fifty years I'm sure you've weathered many storms, Don, so we at Balloons & Tunes thought it only fitting to get you weathered balloons and a weathered old monkey. And now a little poem." He clears his throat, and recites a sonnet he has written and memorized for the occasion. "It all began on a factory floor, a young man, a new life, toothpaste galore . . ."

People smile and chuckle at the rhymes and applaud wildly at the end.

"Thank you, thank you," Kupzyk says. "And now a classic song that has been requested by your coworkers, the ones who truly love you." Kupzyk presses the microphone into the latex mask and begins singing. "No-o cares. No strings. My heart has wings." He raises his arms up and does a pirouette. "If I am fancy free, do doot doot! And love to wander, do do doot! It's just the gypsy in my soul."

As he moves he loses focus, unable to see through the eyeholes of the mask. But he knows people are surprised by his control and elegance. He has practiced for years to achieve this grace. Day after day, month after month. Jazz, tap, modern, ballet, hip-hop. The hours spent in musty studios trying to attain balance in an *arabesque*, power in the *stag leap*. He has sacrificed sunny afternoons at the beach, camping trips, sleepovers. But now he can hear people laughing, and the demanding faces of his dance instructors flash in his mind—Mrs. T. with a cigarette in her wrinkled lips, Mr. Loach on his knees slapping the floor, shouting like a drill sergeant.

Kupzyk stops singing and catches a glimpse of faces laughing at him. He drops the microphone, a deep thud followed by a screech, and he's off, free, leaping, shimmying, turning, sliding, rolling, gyrating, spinning, showing these people, these factory workers, box stuffers, secretaries, supervisors, whatever they are, that even without music this monkey can dance. The laughing stops. And with the exception of his latex feet on the floor and the occasional dish rattling on a nearby table, the room is now silent. Kupzyk leaps, spins, and rolls throughout the large banquet room, ending up on top of an empty table in front of the crowd, where he taps and stomps before ending the show with a *jump over the log*, where he leaps off the table with his left foot and spins in midair, landing on the floor with his right foot.

But while in the air he realizes that he's overcompensated, he has tried too hard, spinning too fast ("Always your problem," Mr. Loach used to say. "Just relax, let it happen!"), and he knows there is no way to correct it. When he hits the floor, his ankle rolls over, off the outside of his foot. He spins out and falls onto his side, grabbing his ankle as the pain burns up his leg.

After a moment people gather around, peering down at him, asking if he's okay. He looks up at their concerned faces and clenches his teeth.

"I'm all right," he says. "I'm all right." He hops up, putting all of his weight on his left leg. "To you, Don!" he shouts, trying to catch his breath. "To you!"

He performs a sweeping bow. The people in the crowd look around at each other and give a tentative applause.

"Congratulations," he says, his ankle searing. "Good luck to you. I hope you have a wonderful new adventure." As he says this, he feels moved. By what, he doesn't know. But there's a tightness in his throat. The old man's forced smile, the crowd's smattering of applause, the sound of his own desperate voice muffled inside the mask, his throbbing ankle, all this sickens him.

He turns and limps toward the door. People converge, smiling, asking if he needs help. He struggles to get through the crowd, hearing the slap of their hands patting him on his wet shoulder, and their voices, distant through the latex mask.

"Wow. Did you see that?"

"Unbelievable."

"That was just great."

He gets outside and hobbles to the far end of the parking lot. The rain has let up a bit. Now a sheer mist is falling. Unable to breathe, he rips off the mask. A bead of sweat falls from his eyebrow and stings his right eye. He squats onto his left leg, as steamy breath billows from his mouth. In a puddle below, a blurry figure looks up at him. Traffic is humming on the nearby freeway. Everyone is going somewhere, he thinks. If you don't like where you are, you can just leave. He thinks about that for a moment. The idea has been milling around in his head for the last few days. But now he forms the words and, even more, he makes a logical argument for moving on, for changing his life.

He thinks about his friend Jordy, who dances with the Hubbard Street Dance Troupe in Chicago. He could stay with Jordy for a while, until he finds his own place. Or he could go to Brooklyn and stay with Diana and Charles. They're old friends, aren't they? The royal couple, as everyone called them. They'd let him sleep on a couch. He could audition for Paul Taylor and Merce Cunningham. He could be a dancer in New York. He'd do Broadway. He'd tour!

He thinks of Don, holding the balloons, as if the balloons themselves were the only things keeping him up, and all the years, a half-century of monotony. How did he do it?

Kupzyk catches his breath and puts his head in his hands, looking down at his reflection in the puddle. "If I am fancy free," he says, "and love to wander."

As he limps back into town, he forms the plan that will take him somewhere else. He'll go home and without saying a word to anyone, he'll get out of his monkey costume and pack a bag with just the essentials. He'll take several aspirin, and then limp out to the highway and stick his thumb into the air. In a few hours he'll be in Chicago, or if he feels like it, he'll continue on to New York. Tomorrow he could be walking down Broadway, in a throng of people, people from all over the world, under those bright lights.

When he gets home, he steps through the front door and sees his six-year-old daughter, Colleen, sitting on an overturned milk crate by the window, reading.

"Hi," she says.

He limps past her, into the bathroom, and flips the light switch. Nothing comes on. "What?" he says, noticing for the first time that the entire apartment is lit only by the gray light that floods through the windows. "Shit." He leans over the sink and searches the dark medicine cabinet for the aspirin.

"What happened to your leg?" Colleen says.

The pain has squirmed all the way up his body and is now pulsing at his temples. His fingers move over the tube of toothpaste, the nail polishes, the lotions, and the hair gels and sprays. "Where is it?" he says. "Are we out of aspirin?"

He limps out to the living room. "Do you know where the bottle of aspirin is?"

Colleen shakes her heard, her eyes still on the book. "Why do you need aspirin?"

"My leg."

"What happened?"

Kupzyk stares down at her, thinking about going into the bedroom, ripping off his costume, grabbing his bag from the closet and stuffing it with clothes.

"Daddy?" she says. "You're drifting off again."

"Huh?" he says. "Oh, I twisted my ankle."

There is a long silence, as Kupzyk leans on his left leg, as if stuck in place. In his mind, he sees his thumb in the air, a green SUV pulling onto the side of the road. He sees himself climbing in.

"How was school today?" he asks, the same question he asks every day.

She shrugs, her eyes still fixed on the book.

He imagines walking around the streets of New York, watching the street performers in Times Square, buying a hot dog in Central Park. He wonders what the weather is like there today. Is it ever as dreary there as it is here? He looks out the window at the rain filling up the neighbor's rowboat beside their house. The water is dark, full of leaves and pine cones. He thinks about the morning Hannah came to his dorm in the spring semester of his freshman year—her hands shaking, her eyes filling with tears—and how he told her that no matter what she decided, he would stand by her, he would do the right thing. He remembers the day of the wedding, the white, plastic chairs on the grass and the humidity pressing on him as he stood there in front of the willow tree in City Park.

"What are you reading?" he asks.

Colleen holds up *The Stranger*, by Camus.

"That's kind of a hard book for you, isn't it?"

"I just like looking for words I can recognize," she says.

"Hm." He peers into the kitchen. "Where's Mom?"

"She went somewhere to try and get the electricity turned back on."

He imagines Hannah—her thin, blond hair soaked and sticking to her scalp—trudging through the rain to the electric company and pleading with the woman behind the glass panel.

Colleen turns a page and scrutinizes some more words. "Dizzy," she reads. "Account."

He sits down on the floor in front of her, taking the pressure off his right leg. He watches her eyes move from word to word, and thinks of last summer, teaching her to read, how the words squeezing out of her tiny mouth thrilled him.

"What were you doing today?" she asks.

"I was a gorilla for somebody's party."

"Like the clown Natalia had for her birthday?"

"Something like that."

She sets the book down and takes the mask from his lap. "Ooo, it's wet."

"Here," he says, shaking it. Water scatters onto the floor. "There you go."

She raises it up and pulls it onto her head. Her blue eyes peek out at him through the little eyeholes. She lifts her arms and scratches her armpits. "*Ooga! Ooga! Ooga!*" she says.

She stands up and swings her arms back and forth across her knees, and grunts a few times. "It's hard to see in here," she says.

He has to get out. If he's ever going to leave, it has to be now. He thinks about the stop sign. If only he hadn't run that stop sign, it'd be so much easier. He could just hop in his car now and be in New York by tomorrow. Hell, he could go in the opposite direction. He could go to Seattle if he wanted, or San Francisco, if the car would make it. He imagines the Chevette, locked up in an impound lot on the outskirts of town, sitting there in a row of other cars, hundreds and hundreds of cars all waiting there in the rain.

Colleen sits back down. "How can you breathe in this thing?"

"Colleen," he says, leaning forward and grabbing her, squeezing her small body into his furry arms. The latex twists around her face and shrivels between them.

"You're cold," she says, her voice garbled in the mask.

He pulls it off and kisses the top of her head. She eases into him and lets him hold her. They sit like this for a moment, before Kupzyk realizes he's still holding on to the mask. He opens his fingers and lets it go, and then he straightens Colleen's messy hair, trying to ignore the sharp pain in his ankle.

The rain is coming down harder now, and he wonders if Hannah is all right out there. He hopes that she took an umbrella with her, a raincoat, the proper boots.

Maybe he'll sit like this for while with Colleen in his hairy arms. He'll sit with her, feeling her rib cage move with each breath. And they might talk for a bit—about what, he doesn't know, but he'll hold her—and they'll sit here together, and they'll wait. Pretty soon the lights will turn back on.

"How does it go?" he asks. "What's a monkey do?"

"Well, first," she says, "you scratch yourself, and you make a funny face. And then you go, *Ooga, ooga. ooga.*"

"Oh," he says.

Immigration

When the phone rang I knew another car had been stolen. Third one in two months. I knew it, and I didn't bother answering it.

It was a little after one in the morning. I rolled out of bed, walked into the bathroom, and took two aspirin. As the date of our trip got closer, the headaches got worse. My wife and I hadn't really traveled since our honeymoon, and so twenty years later, for our anniversary, we were going on a second one. This time to Disney World, "a place," my wife had said, "that has an international section where we can feel as if we're in any country in the world."

The phone kept ringing.

I looked in the mirror and noticed that my hair had stopped falling out. "In waves," the doctor had said. "It comes and goes." I lowered my head and began fingering through the thin strands of hair, looking for new fuzz on my scalp. The ringing stopped. I heard Jennifer's voice in a low grumble, "Hello?" And then she said, "Harry, it's for you."

I looked up at myself, at the wrinkles forming around my eyes. "Tell them I'm not here."

"It's someone from the security company."

"I know, I know, I know." I walked back into the bedroom and sat on the bed, wondering what they took, an Altima, or a Murano. I hunched over and put my head in my hands. Jennifer tapped my shoulder with the phone.

I took it from her and put it to my ear. "Hello?"

I met my wife when I was fifteen up north in Monte Cristo, where the Stilliguamash falls from the Cascades and begins its twisting path to the Puget Sound. Her family was camping on Lake Myrtle, mine on Lost Lake. One day I was out hiking by myself when I saw a boy about my age standing on the edge of Lake Myrtle, fly-fishing. I went over to watch him. He was taller than me and had long, muscular arms and straight blond hair. He knew I was watching him and without looking at me he said, "What are you looking at?"

"Nothing," I said.

He stopped whipping his rod, letting the fly land on the lake's smooth surface. "Good. Keep it that way," he said.

In his right hand he held the long bamboo pole. He curled his left index finger around the line and slowly pulled it away from his body, all the time concentrating on the fly drifting on the water. But then he turned to me and smiled.

After I hung up I threw on some clothes and left of the house. It was a warm night but the streets were wet from rain that fell earlier.

The lady at the security company said it wasn't a stolen car, just some kids throwing rocks and spraying graffiti on the fence.

At any rate I had to go down to the lot to turn off the alarm. There were a few scattered clouds in the sky, but it was mostly clear. Above Lake Union the faint, red glow of Mars was making its way through the darkness below Ursa Minor. Cassiopeia lay off to the East, above Lake Washington.

As I got closer to the lot, I could hear the cry of the alarm. Graffiti covered the fence in blues and reds, words and phrases I couldn't read. I pulled out my keys and unlocked the gate. The *Universal-Rent-A-Car* sign had been shattered, but inside everything was fine. The cars I hadn't rented that day were still there and in good condition and the office looked untouched. I punched the code word into the alarm system, "*Jupiter.*"

Silence.

It was the night before our twentieth anniversary, and the next day we were going to fly across the country to look at artificial societies. I leaned back against a silver Sentra and thought about how slowly time had passed, and how easy it was for me to remember events I had previously forgotten, as if a magician had pulled up a silky red scarf and made them appear out of the thin air.

I looked over at my business, at what I owned. I didn't finish the paint job in time for the Fourth of July, so the awning was half hearts, half stars. The hearts were from the big Valentine's Day promotion, which didn't turn the profit we thought it would, and the stars in red, white, and blue were for Independence Day. We got so busy I couldn't finish and didn't really need to. So many people needed to rent cars for the weekend, they didn't seem to care what was painted on the building.

• • •

The tall boy kept smiling at me. "What's your name?" he said.

I looked out at the lake. "Harry."

He closed his mouth and shook his head. "Harry. Harry what?"

"Oh, uh, Flowers," I said.

He started reeling in his line. "Harry Flowers," he said. And then he laughed. He said his name was Charlie Person, and if I laughed he'd punch me.

"Why would I laugh?"

"Cuz, Person, it's what I am. You know, it's like having a dog and naming it Dog," he said.

He took me back to his campsite and introduced me to his mother and father and his little sister, who were all sitting at a picnic table playing cards. It turned out that they lived only a couple miles from my family in Seattle, and that we'd both be starting up at Roosevelt High School in the fall.

I spent the rest of the camping trip playing with Charlie. He taught me how to fly fish and I taught him how to swim. I was amazed that somebody that muscular and athletic could only manage a simple dog paddle.

"Do you promise not to tell anybody?" he asked.

I nodded. "Yeah, sure."

"Okay," he said, "I've uh . . ." He looked away from me and then down at his hands that swirled in the water around his hips. "I've always been a little afraid to put my head under."

We became best friends. He was the basketball star, and I was the towel boy. He was the homecoming king and I took pictures of him for the yearbook. When his little sister started coming over to my house to baby-sit my little sister, everybody said, "Harry and Jennifer would make a good couple." They said it so much that without any effort at all we ended up together.

After Charlie and I graduated, we roomed together at the University of Washington, where he walked on to the basketball team, and I spent most of my time bowling down at the Hub. After one year my grades were so bad, I decided to enroll in technical school and ask Jennifer to marry me. Three months later, after the wedding, we moved into a small two-bedroom house by Northgate. I got a certificate to repair electronics—ham radios, TVs, hair dryers and toasters—and started working for an old man named Mr. Guftafson (I never knew his first name) in a small shop in Ballard. And then one day I came home from work and Jennifer burst out of the house, rubbing her eyes with the back of her hand. She came up to the side of the car and threw her arms around me as I got out.

"What's wrong, honey?"

"I can't believe it," she said. "We weren't even trying."

"What are you talking about?"

"Harry." She pulled away from me, her eyes puffy and bloodshot.

That night I watched her fall asleep—her body curled up like a little girl—with a John Cougar song playing on the radio. I thought about how irreversible it all is, how there is no way to go back and start again. I got up, put on my robe, and went outside.

It was a clear night, and the constellation Perseus hung low in the sky just to the north. I tried to remember what I had studied in astronomy, the only class I enjoyed in college, about the variable star, Algol, how every three days or so it loses its brightness for five hours as it goes behind another smaller star. I propped myself up on the hood of our Impala and tried to make out the entire figure of Perseus with the sword above his head and Medusa's skull in his outstretched hand.

Nine months later a storm moved in. I got up in the middle of the night and sat down at the dining room table. Outside, thick snowflakes blew down from the sky and spread themselves out over our backyard. I watched them fall, wishing I could sleep, hoping they would hypnotize me in some way, make me drowsy. But then I felt my wife's hand on my shoulder. "Harry, honey? Harry? It's starting."

Mars has two small moons. I looked up and tried to remember their names. I pulled out my keys and walked past the cars and off the lot. Phoebe? The gate slid closed with relative ease, and this time the key didn't get stuck in the lock. I knew one started with a P.

Penelope? I made a note in my head to tell my son Damon to paint over the graffiti on the fence while his mother and I were away—Damon, my pot-smoking genius of a son, the one I caught at fifteen pulling two plastic bags of dope out of his socks right in front of his baby sister, and the one who cried as I washed them down the garbage disposal in the kitchen sink. Later that night I got up to get a glass of milk and there he was, his long skinny body on the kitchen floor, his head under the sink, a screwdriver in one hand and a wrench in the other. Spread out around his legs were washers, nuts, and a couple of short silver pipes.

Right then I thought of what my father said to me when I was a kid. He said, "My great grandfather Fargus came to America from Scotland in 1874, and with his sperm, he gave birth to a long line of alcoholics and underachievers. Listen to me, boy. The

Flowers will never bloom." He was usually drunk when he said this, so I rarely listened.

One time I said, "But Grampa ran for mayor."

"Yeah," he said, "and lost."

My grampa got sober when he turned sixty and spent the rest of his life in back alleys and skid row hotels, helping the homeless.

Maybe my father was right about us. After all, his father helped bums, and he himself was certainly below that, a car salesman, and I was yet a step below that, a car renter. I figured we were just working our way down the ladder, and my son will complete the natural progression: he'll probably end up a bum.

I hiked up Pike Street, wondering about the mind, the way it lets things in for a while and then dismisses them. Why couldn't I remember certain things I had learned when I was young, yet remembered silly things my father had said? How I could forget the two moons of Mars?

Up the street I could see the redbrick buildings of the community college, and was thinking about maybe taking a class there, when I heard a whimpering sound from behind the trees outside the theater building.

"Hello?" I said. "Hello?"

I walked off the sidewalk and into the little courtyard toward the bronze fountain of angels. The rhododendrons were in bloom, and the fountain was turned off, and the three angels above me, their wings jutting out from their backs, looked like they were about to fly away.

"Hello?" I said.

The weeping continued, but I couldn't see where it was coming from. I worked my way around the fountain and crouched down to peer into the bushes. To my right, under a long wooden bench, a leg moved. I got down on my hands and knees and crawled towards it.

"Hello?" I said. "You okay?"

"What?" I asked. "What did you say?"

She stood there, staring down at me, in a pink sweatshirt, with her hair pulled back. "I think it's starting, Harry." She was hugging a heart shaped pillow.

"What's starting?"

"My labor, honey."

"What?"

"My labor. The contractions are coming really fast."

"Um, okay!" I rushed into the bedroom, threw on my robe, and ran out the front door. It was dark and the snow was falling hard. I hopped into the Impala and cranked the key in the ignition. I turned on the heater and the windshield wipers, and then I jumped out and ran back into the house. Jennifer was on the couch in the living room.

"Harry," she said. "Don't panic. It'll be all right."

I stopped and looked down at her. "What?" I said. And then, I don't know why, but I started to cry.

"Oh, honey," she said, hoisting herself up. "Honey?" She began rubbing the back of my neck. "Babe, what is it?"

"I just . . . I don't know. I don't think . . ." I said. There was silence, and I could feel her staring at me.

"What, honey?" she said, "What is it?"

I shook my head, turned away and went into the bedroom.

"What were you going to say, honey? You just don't think what?"

"Nothing!" I said. I grabbed a pair of pants from the dresser and pulled them on.

She walked into the room. "What were you going to say?"

"Nothing," I said, zipping up my pants. "I got a little emotional. That's all."

"Harry."

I bent down and slipped on my shoes.

"You're not communicating again," she said. "Just talk to me."

"Honey, we have to get you to the hospital."

"Harry, I understand if you're scared, but will you just talk to me? Remember, we said we'd talk about things. You said your weren't going to keep stuff bottled up anymore."

"Jesus, would you listen to this? Can we just get going?"

She straightened up, her little arms squeezing the pillow to her chest. "Harry? Do you want this baby?"

"Oh, tell me you're kidding."

"You can be honest," she said.

"Can we get out of here?"

"Harry, you don't want this baby, do you?"

I slipped my jacket on. "Honey, for God's sake, will you listen to yourself? Of course I do."

"You haven't touched me in weeks, Harry," she said. "I know you're not happy."

"Honey this is not the time to be talking about this."

"When should we talk, Harry? Huh? You tell me when, okay? Just let me know when you'd like to discuss this."

She stood there, waiting for me to say something. Nothing was coming out. I wanted to tell her I was sorry. But I didn't know what for. I zipped my jacket and walked out of the room. She followed me into the hallway.

"When the baby's in my arms?" she said. "When it's breast-feeding? Is that when you'd like to talk about it, Harry? When it's asleep in the other room? When it's two years old? Fourteen? When it's graduating from high school? How about that, huh? Our little boy up there, getting his diploma, and Harry finally wants to talk about how he didn't want this baby." Her face was flushed, and spit was flying out of her mouth. "When do you think we should talk, Harry?"

"Honey," I said, "You're doing it again, okay? Let's just, please, forget all this and get you to the hospital."

She took a deep breath and said, "Why'd you marry me?"

"What?"

"I mean, you married me, Harry. You did this to me. Now you don't want this baby? It's a little late, Harry! Don't you think it's a little late?" Her chin started to quiver and her lips tightened.

"Don't be so theatrical," I said. "This isn't one of your high school plays!"

"Excuse me?"

"Well, you're just . . . you're getting all crazy."

"What? You said you weren't going to use that word again."

"Look," I said, putting my hands on her shoulders. "Just calm down, all right?"

"Don't touch me, you son-of-a-bitch." She turned and went into the bathroom and slammed the door.

"Honey, come on now!" I grabbed the knob. It was locked. "Oh, Jesus, Jennifer."

She was crying, sucking in deep breaths.

"Please?" I said. "Would you open the door?"

"You're the husband," she said.

"Yes, I am."

"You're supposed to support me, but you don't want to talk. You never want to talk. And then you cry and say you don't want the baby."

"I didn't say that!"

"Yes, you did!"

"Listen, goddammit! I want the damn baby! Now get the hell out of there so we can go! I'm not playing any more stupid games. Get out here right now!"

She screamed—a sound I had never heard before—and then it was silent.

"Honey, are you okay?" I asked.

On the other side of the door I could hear her doing her breathing. In, two, three. Out, two, three.

"Are you all right?"

"They're getting close," she said.

"Okay, Jennifer? I'm going out to the car now. All right? I'm going to the car. If you want to go to the hospital, that's where I'll be."

She opened the bathroom door and looked up at me. "No you won't, goddammit," she said, "You're going to take me by the hand, and you are going to escort me out of this house down the steps and into the car! We're going to do this right."

We made it out into the falling snow, down the sidewalk, and to the side of the Impala. Steam shot out of her mouth in quick, successive puffs. I tried to open the passenger door, but it was locked. "I'll be right back, honey," I said. I ran around to the driver's side, grabbed the handle, and pulled on the door. It didn't open.

"Shit," I said.

"What is it, Harry?" Jennifer asked.

I looked down through the window. "Oh no," I said, looking over the car. Her head was covered with snow.

"Harry? What is it?"

"Nothing, honey," I said. "I'll be right back." I turned and ran around to the side yard.

"Harry!" she yelled. "Harry!"

I grabbed a shovel that was leaning against the fence. Snow fell in my eyes as I rounded the house. I rushed up to the car with the shovel over my shoulder like a baseball bat.

"Honey," I said, "look out." I closed my eyes and swung at the driver side window. Glass exploded everywhere, flying against my face and hands.

"Harry, are you okay?" she said.

I unlocked the door and pulled it open. It was warm inside the car, where the heater blew out a constant gust of stale, hot air. I leaned across and opened her door.

"Hold on a second, honey!" I said, wiping the shards of glass off the seat, one sticking into my ring finger.

Jennifer slowly sat down, her legs still outside the car, snow melting in her hair.

I ran around to her side, pulling the piece of glass from my finger. I put my hands under her knees and lifted her legs up. She swiveled her body around and placed her feet on the floor.

"You okay, honey? You comfortable?" I asked.

She nodded, sniffed, and wiped her eyes with the back of her hand. I closed the door, ran around to my side, and climbed into the car.

"Oh!" she cried, and then started in on her breathing. *Hu, hu, hee. Hu, hu, hee.*

I pulled out of the driveway. Snow blew through my broken window onto my shoulder and my legs. Blood dripped from my finger, down the steering wheel and into my lap. The streets were slick, but I drove quickly, skillfully, trying to make up for the fiasco I had just made of my life.

I thought of my grampa as I crawled up to the bench, how he did this for the last few years of his life, every night with the homeless. But as I got closer, I noticed that the young man under the bench didn't look homeless. He was wearing clean khaki trousers and leather dress shoes. I got up, walked around to the back of the bench, and crouched down to look at him. He lay on his side, asleep or passed out, his arms hugging his chest. His eyes were swollen and bruised. I moved my fingers around his neck until I found a pulse. Blood dripped from his open mouth, and there was a deep cut on his cheek.

I bent down, lifted him into my arms, and carried him past the fountain, under the trees and onto the sidewalk. No cars were coming down Broadway, so I jaywalked and made my way through the shadowy streets to Thirteenth with the stranger in my arms.

The house was dark and quiet. I carried him through the kitchen and set him on the rec room floor. I went into the bathroom, and put a clean washrag under running water. He was still asleep when I came in and eased myself down beside him. As I started to wipe the cut on his cheek, he said in a strange accent, "George. George." His breath reeked of alcohol. I stopped and looked into his bloody mouth. "George."

I went back into the bathroom and pulled a gauze pad and medical tape out of the cabinet. The bleeding on his cheek had slowed, but I put the pad on anyway.

"Dee cloration" he muttered. "Dee cloration."

I took off his shoes. He wasn't wearing any socks and his toes were callused.

The kitchen light turned on. "Harry?" Jennifer whispered. "What's going on?"

"Don't worry, honey," I said. "Go back to bed."

"Who is that?"

I got up and walked into the kitchen.

"I thought you were a burglar," she said. "All this noise in the dark. Who is that?"

I opened the refrigerator. "You want anything?" I asked.

"Was he the one?" she said. "Down at the lot?"

I pulled out a carton of milk. "No," I said. "I found him under a bench."

"What?"

Tammy, our fifteen-year-old daughter, came into the kitchen. She was wearing plaid boxer shorts and a T-shirt that said *Don't Bother.* "Hey, guys, what's happening?"

Jennifer turned to her. "Tammy, go back to bed."

"Who's that?" Tammy asked.

"It's none of your business, honey, now scoot," Jennifer said.

"What do you mean it's none of my business?" Tammy said. "This is my house too."

"He's just a man I found," I said. "He was kinda beat up."

"Cool, Dad. And you saved him?"

I poured the milk into a glass. "Well, not really, honey. But your mom is right. You need to go up to your room now and go back to sleep. It's late. I'll tell you about it in the morning."

"Dad," she whined.

"It's almost three o'clock. Now go back to bed."

"I'm not sleeping anyway," she said. "I've been reading this whole time. Kafka!"

"Tammy," Jennifer said.

"It's crazy."

"Well, good," I said. "Go back and finish your crazy book then."

She gave me a look and went upstairs. I sat down at the table and sipped my milk. Jennifer sat down across from me.

"We're leaving tomorrow morning, you know?" she said.

"Don't worry, I'll get plenty of sleep on the plane."

"And what do you plan to do with him?" she asked.

"Jennifer. He was hurt, on the street. He needed help."

"Why didn't you just call an ambulance?"

"It's not that bad, just a black eye and a couple bruises." I gulped down my milk.

"What if he steals, or something? It's not safe bringing a stranger in here."

"I tell you what . . ." I said.

"No, really, what were you thinking?"

"I'll sit up and watch him. Okay? And then as soon as he wakes up, I'll make him leave."

"I don't know about you," she said. "I really don't."

"Why don't you go up and get some sleep?"

"I don't know if I can," she said.

"Honey," I said.

"How was the lot?" she asked.

"Oh. Just graffiti. Damon can paint over it when we're gone."

Jennifer got up and took the empty glass out of my hands and put it in the sink. "Now I'm going back to bed," she said. "Can you please get him out of here, now?"

I nodded. "All right."

She gave me a pouty half smile, and said, "I don't know about you." And then she walked out of the room. I listened to her slippered feet climbing the stairs. Our bedroom door clicked shut.

The fluorescent light flickered above me. I got up, turned it off, and went into the rec room, where the man still slept. What was I going to do, pick him back up and carry him out to the street? It was probably going to start raining soon.

I grabbed a blanket from the hall cabinet and draped it over him, and then sat down and watched him. He was small, trim, kind of muscular. He had high cheekbones and a long nose. His chin was square, with a little cleft in the middle.

The house was still again. I wondered what he was going to make of all this, sleeping in a strange house, waking to a bandaged face and a large man looking down at him.

My thoughts turned to Mars, the planet that changes color in springtime. I tried again to remember its two moons. It was one of the questions on the final in college, the only final I did well on and kept in my scrapbook in the attic. I thought about going up and looking at it. But then it came to me: Phobos. The other one seemed to bark out to me at the same moment: Deimos. I went to the window and looked at the sky, now covered with low white clouds. Phobos and Deimos were up there somewhere.

I turned around and sat down on the floor next to him. He mumbled something in a language I couldn't understand. I reached out slowly and placed my right hand on his shoulder. He rolled over on his side, still sound asleep. I kept my hand on his shoulder. "George," he mumbled. "George Washington."

I felt tired, so I lay down beside him and closed my eyes. I moved my body in close to his until my stomach touched his back. I was on my side, my legs curled up inside his, my head resting on my left arm, my right arm around his tight, solid torso, holding him as if he were about to fall apart. He kept muttering in his sleep. I listened to the low rumbling of his voice for a while and wondered what it would sound like if he said my name. But then he stopped, and I could hear the house creaking. I took a deep breath and began to feel a little dizzy. I took another and then another, filling up my lungs slowly with the smells that rolled off him, cigarette smoke, alcohol, and sweat. I pushed the breath out and felt light and calm. Everything was still. I thought of Mars, its red glow floating way up in the darkness, high above the city. It's just dust that makes it red, I thought, just dust. And then I fell asleep.

At the hospital, complications set in when the doctor discovered that the baby was coming out feet first. They tried frantically to turn him around, and when that didn't work they cut Jennifer open. I was never superstitious, but I just knew from the start that Damon was cursed.

Three years later, Tammy was born without a hitch, and we moved into the University District. I quit my job repairing electronics and became a carpenter, mainly drywall, until my father died of liver poisoning and left me a surprising amount of money. I took some of it and went into rehab to get sober. The rest I invested in my car rental business. We moved to Capitol Hill, so my wife could walk to the New City Theater where she'd begun acting. It worked out well. I could walk to my business, Jennifer was by her theater, and Damon could buy drugs any time he wanted.

One time he actually tried to fight me. It was during Christmas, and some of Jennifer's relatives were up from California. A Bing Crosby song was playing on the stereo. Damon and I started wrestling, just playing around, as everyone watched with glasses of eggnog in their hands. I grabbed him and threw him against the wall. His face turned red, and he threw a punch at me. I ducked and belted him in the stomach. He doubled over, his hands on his belly, and fell onto his knees in front of the fireplace. I looked up at the room full of cousins, aunts, and uncles. "I'm sorry about this, everyone. I'm sorry."

He became a pretty good student and got excellent test scores, despite the drugs, and I began thinking that he might actually become something someday. But in the month that followed graduation, we didn't see him around the house very often. He'd come in when we weren't there, talk to his sister, and then get something to eat. Sometimes he'd grab some clothes and go over to his girlfriend's. So I was surprised when he came home the morning I was lying there asleep with the stranger in my arms.

"Dad?" he said, shaking my shoulder. "Dad?"

I opened my eyes and saw the back of the stranger's head. I looked up at my long-haired son.

"Hey," he said, "What the fuck?"

My neck had a kink in it. I moved my head around, and then rolled over on the floor. "What?" I said.

"What's going on, Dad?" he said.

I ran my hand through my hair, and rubbed my eyes. "Jesus," I said.

"Where's Mom?" he asked.

I jumped up and walked into the kitchen. The gray morning light filtered through the windows. "Huh?" I asked.

"Where's Mom?"

"She's upstairs," I said.

"Who is that guy?"

"Oh, just somebody I found on Broadway. He was beat up pretty bad." I pulled the carton of milk out of the refrigerator. My hand was shaking. "I brought him home to take care of him."

"I can see that," he said. "He looks kind of thrashed."

I tried to yawn, and then leaned back against the counter. "Yeah, well, somebody beat him up. You want some milk?"

"So what's going on Dad, I mean, you found some guy on Broadway? Is he gay?"

"It's nothing," I said. I turned and poured milk into a glass.

"Dad, you had your arm around that guy."

"Oh, yeah, I must have fallen asleep."

"Yeah, well," he said, looking out the window. "You got twenty bucks?"

"What for?"

"Tina and I are going camping today up at Granite Falls, and we need some gas money." He pointed outside. "See, she's out in the car waiting for me."

I looked out the window. Her eyes were closed and she was wearing a black ski cap and a flannel shirt. A thin, silver ring was sticking out of her nose.

"Granite Falls? Come on, Damon, I'm not stupid."

"What are you talking about?"

"That's where all that meth is made."

"Give me a break. It's also got some fine camping and hiking and whatnot. Or have you forgotten that?"

"Damon, please tell me you're not doing meth now."

"Dad, meth is for freaks, okay?"

"Then why don't you just say what you really need the money for?"

"Well, Dad, why don't you tell me what you were doing with your arm around that dude?"

I looked at his skinny body, his pale skin.

The stranger mumbled, "George. George."

Damon turned and walked into the rec room. "Who's George?" he said. "Maybe like a lover or something?"

"I don't know," I said, pulling my wallet out of my pocket. I stretched my arm out with the twenty-dollar bill in my fingers.

He came over and took it from me. "Thanks, Dad. I really appreciate it." He folded the bill and slipped it in his pocket. "Oh, Dad, listen, man, it's a crazy world, man, I know."

"Yeah, crazy," I said.

"But you've, you know, always been cool to me. I mean, I caused you a lot of shit." He turned and pointed down at the man asleep on the floor. "So, it's cool, man. I mean, that's your business, right? I mean, who am I? Who is anybody, you know?"

I took a sip of milk.

"Anyway . . ." He turned and started to leave.

"Damon," I said.

He stopped. I looked across the room at his thin face, the bags under his eyes, and in that one moment I thought, *I've known you your entire life, you little bastard.* I wanted to go over and slap him and then hug him and then slap him again, maybe ball my hand up into a fist and really give him one.

"What, Dad?" he asked.

I looked away from him, out the window, at his skinny girl-friend asleep in the front seat of his car. I felt sorry for them, I couldn't help thinking how much harder they have it than I did, how little hope, and yet how they've managed to remain sweet. "Somebody graffitied the hell out of the fence down at the lot," I said. "Could you take care of that for me while your mom and I are away?"

"Sure thing. Tell Mom I said hi," he said. "Happy anniversary, Dad." He turned and went out the back door. I watched him through the window as he walked to his car, my old car, the '92 Saturn he bought from me for four hundred bucks (four hundred bucks he borrowed from me and never repaid). He opened the door and hopped in. Tina sat up and looked at him and then closed her eyes and leaned her head back against the seat. He put his arm around her, kissed her on the forehead, and pulled out of the driveway.

I went over to the stranger on the floor and nudged him with my foot. "Hey. Hey, buddy. Time to wake up."

"Huh?" he said. He put his hands on his head.

"It's time for you to leave," I said.

He looked around, dazed, and then put his shoes on. He made it to his feet and stumbled to the back door. I followed him outside. He told me, in his thick Eastern European accent, that there were three of them, and they punched him in the face and kicked him in the ribs. I told him he should call the police.

He said, "It was dark. I saw no faces, only bodies."

I walked him down to Broadway. He started telling me about how the day before he'd taken a test and had become an American citizen, and how later that night after drinking with friends he was beaten and thrown to the ground for no apparent reason. And then he said, "I'm free. I'm a free man."

I brought him to the courtyard where I'd found him just a few hours earlier. The fountain was on, and water fell from the angels' mouths. I helped him sit down on the bench and asked him if he was going to be okay.

"Oh, thank you," he said. "You are kind. Sit with me. Talk with me."

"No, I can't," I said. "I have to get back. Can you get home from here?"

He put his hand on his stomach and coughed. He looked at me and said, "What is your name?"

I looked up at the fountain and then beyond that, at the cars on the street. A long white limousine drove by. "I'm Harry," I said.

He reached his hand out to me. "Zbigniew."

I shook his hand. "It's a pleasure," I said.

He smiled at me. "Harry."

"Yep, Harry," I said.

"Like Harry Potter?"

"I guess so."

"Do you know magic, Harry?"

I chuckled and said, "I don't know." I stood there looking at him looking back at me. I knew something more needed to be said, but I couldn't think of anything.

I turned and walked to the corner and started to cross the street. But halfway across I stopped and looked back over my shoulder at him, at Zbigniew. He had a smile on his bruised and beaten face as he looked up at the angels. A car honked at me and then another and another. The crosswalk said *Don't Walk*. I was standing in the middle of an intersection with cars all around me.

On the plane to Florida, I tried to sleep, but Jennifer kept asking me about him. "Poor guy, comes to America and gets beat up. What else did he say?"

"Just that he came to Seattle to repair boats and ended up staying ten years," I said, putting a pillow behind my head.

"That's it?" she asked. "What kind of boats?"

"Down at Lockheed or something. I don't know. I didn't talk to him that long." I pushed the button on the arm of the seat and reclined. "But he said he was free. That he'd passed the test, and he was free."

"What test?" Jennifer asked.

A flight attendant leaned over Jennifer's shoulder. "Would you all like anything to drink?" she asked.

"I'm fine," I said.

"Can I have a glass of orange juice?" Jennifer said.

It was a muggy evening when we landed in Florida. A Cuban man with a thick accent carried our bags up to our room. I gave him a five-dollar tip, which Jennifer said was too much.

The air-conditioning was on and the room was cool. I sat down on the bed and started unbuttoning my shirt. I pulled the covers away from the headboard. Jennifer was humming a song in the shower. I imagined her, the woman I had known since I was fifteen years old, washing her short, brown hair, running the bar of soap over her kneecaps, and across her purple-veined thighs. I thought about how well we knew each other. As well as anybody could, I thought.

I thought of Zbigniew, his bloody face and callused toes, and how he smiled when he said my name. I took my shirt off, crawled into bed and pulled the covers over my face. Everything turned black—a deep, wide patch of darkness, like the night sky. But this time I wasn't looking up at it. I was inside it, a star, or a planet, way out there in the dark, alone, making my way across the cosmos. And I wondered what my moons would be called, or if I even had any. I imagined people on some faraway planet looking up and seeing me shine in their dark sky. What would they say? Or would they notice? There is so much to see, and still so much space between it all, so much darkness. I closed my eyes and felt myself spin through the universe. I was in orbit.

Karrooo

I'm heading west on I-80 with my two teenagers, Paul and Allison. We've been in the car for almost six hours now, and we've settled into our own remote worlds—Allison with her walkman, me with the radio, and Paul still playing that computer game in the back seat. Occasionally he blurts out, "Come on," or "Oh no," his thumbs smacking at the little plastic keys.

Paul is a thirteen-year-old with blotchy skin and an extra thirty pounds that started accumulating when his father got an apartment in the city last year. He can't seem to bring a positive thought to completion. He may start with the sun shining in a bright blue sky but somehow he works his way down into a mosquito-ridden mud puddle. "Yeah, Trevor invited me to his party, but it's only because you're friends with his mom." That sort of thing.

Allison, my too-good-to-be-true sixteen-year-old, is listening to *Henry IV Part I* on her walkman. She says she's in love with Prince Hal. With every new play she loses herself in the great tempest of passion for some heroic, romantic character, who (she'll realize soon enough) will never, without a doubt, exist on this planet.

The Platte River moves lazily under us as we cross a bridge in the fading evening sun. The river doesn't care about where it's heading or when it needs to get there. Like the people of this state, the Platte is not against meandering and low expectations. That's why I escaped, I suppose. I was focused and ambitious, which of course led to a whole host of other problems.

I left Grand Island at seventeen, with my National Merit Scholarship, to attend Grinnell, before interning in DC for Senator Harkin and partying with so-called important people and people hoping to become important-policy makers, bribe takers, martini shakers, in that order, and me, all twenty-two ambitious years of me. I didn't know then that I'd end up a frustrated non-profit administrator unsuccessfully married to a college professor with whom I'd have two kids who sometimes call me by my first name.

On the other side of the Platte, railroad tracks scoot under the freeway and wind along the riverside. I think of my father, who traveled along those tracks for almost forty years, all the time wishing he could be in the sky.

When he was nineteen he joined the Air Force, but his vision wasn't good enough to fly, so they stuck him in Sacramento for two years, running a maintenance shop. From there he moved back home and got a job on the Burlington-Northern. He once told me that he spent all his downtime leaning out of the train, looking up at the sky and the hawks and eagles circling above.

The idea of flight fascinated him. Walking on the wind, he called it. Before long he became an avid bird-watcher, joining the Audubon Society, heading out on his days off with his friends Bernie and Len.

I remember him once waking me in the middle of the night. "Linda, dear," he said, standing over me.

It was the day after Thanksgiving, and he'd just received a phone call from someone at the American Birding Association. A yellow grosbeak had been spotted feeding at a corn silo outside Ottumwa.

"I don't want to go, Daddy," I said. "Take Len."

"He can't make it," he whispered. "Listen, this is extraordinary, honey. The yellow grosbeak is a tropical bird. It never makes it north of Houston, for God's sake."

"Daddy," I said. "I'm tired."

He was a dark blob, his large body silhouetted by the dim hall light. "I just didn't want you to miss something like this." He backed up and stopped at the door. "I'm sorry I woke you," he said, before turning and heading to central Iowa for what was to become one of the great bird outings of his life.

He returned the next afternoon reeling from the sight of that grosbeak, and something unexpected. On the way home he pulled off at a rest stop where he spotted a lone duck on a small pond shaded by poplars. He rushed back to the pickup and grabbed his binoculars.

"You won't guess what it was," he said that evening at the dinner table. "I mean, I thought it was just a common duck. But it wasn't. It was a red-breasted merganser. I couldn't believe it. It must have been up from the Gulf or down from the Great Lakes or something, because I'll tell you, there are never red-breasted mergansers in Nebraska, ever. They're saltwater birds. But there he was, gliding around, looking for food. He was male, with the green head, you know, and just a beautiful rust-colored breast, and his beak was just a bright, bright red."

I didn't know it at the time, but my father was fast approaching what is known as the 700 Club, an exclusive group of birders who have spotted more than 700 North American species. In the years that followed, when I was off in Grinnell, DC, and then St. Paul, my eventual home, my father was tromping through marshlands and rocky hillsides from the Aleutians to Newfoundland, adding to his impressive list of rare bird sightings. To date he has spotted and identified an approved 739 species of birds. But my mother's death and his heart attacks slowed him down. His trips became shorter, and he had to be content traipsing around Lake McConaughy, or the south fork of the Platte, no longer finding new birds, but enjoying the birds he'd seen hundreds of times before.

A couple hours later, after passing through Lincoln, with its phallic capitol building rising into the sky, and the small town of York, where there's a water tower that's painted like a hot-air balloon, I turn off the freeway onto the Tom Osborne Expressway, littered with the bright lights of fast-food restaurants, glorified five-and-dimes, auto-parts stores, and home-improvement warehouses. From there I wind through the new downtown toward the neighborhood I was raised in, a few blocks behind the old downtown, on an old street lined with oak and some sort of elm that is dying from an incurable disease.

When I pull into the driveway, the thought hits me that this might be the last time I see this place, the last time my feet will sink into this sod, the last time I'll climb these steps to the porch where I received my first kiss. And ringing the doorbell on the house I've always called home, I'm immediately worried that my father won't know who I am.

"What exactly is a stroke?" Paul asks.

"Paul," Allison says, "we've already been through that."

"Yeah, but it doesn't make any sense. Why do they call it a stroke? It's not like he's swimming or anything."

The door opens, and Marcella, in a long gray shawl, raises a wilted hand in the air, expecting me to embrace her. "Linda," she says. "How are you?"

I step inside and we hug for a moment before she moves back and asks to take our coats, as if we're first-time houseguests arriving late for a dinner party. Paul and Allison lumber in, and Paul stands there with all the enthusiasm of a fence board.

"Don't worry about that, Grandma M," Allison says. "I'll hang up our coats."

"Well, that's wonderful," Marcella says. I try to picture her as a nun (her profession for almost thirty-five years before meeting my father at the hospital after his last heart attack) and I can see it—the ruler in her hand and the hard, lifeless expression, as if etched on her face by Grant Wood himself.

"How is he?" I ask.

"He is doing just fine. Everything is fine."

"Can we go say hi to him?" Allison says, wrapping her jacket around a hanger.

Marcella frowns and pushes out a sigh. "I'm afraid it's a bit late and we don't want to wake him."

"We'll be quiet," Paul says.

"Tomorrow," Marcella says. "After a good night's rest."

"Marcella," I say, "we've driven a long way. All we want to do is peek in and say hi."

"But he's sleeping," she says. "Tomorrow, after he wakes up, you can spend the whole day with him."

. . .

After Paul eats some leftover spaghetti, he sets up a makeshift bed on the living room couch and plugs in his video game called Warlord, or Warlock, or something with "War" in it. Allison and I unpack upstairs in what used to be my bedroom, now Marcella's crafting room with rolls of bright and busy material leaning in the corner beside my mother's '54 Singer.

Allison is chattering on and on as we take the boxes Marcella has heaped on my old double bed and stack them by the bureau in the corner. And just who would she choose?

"Whom," I say. "*Whom* would you choose?"

"Prince Hal or Hotspur?" she says. "I mean, if I was confronted with a choice like that."

"*Were* confronted," I say, opening my suitcase. "And just a piece of advice you probably won't listen to. I've been with the Hals and the Hotspurs of the world, and if I were you, I'd be looking for a Falstaff."

"What?" she says. "He's old and fat."

"But he'll make you laugh."

"I'll be in the bathroom," she says, grabbing her toiletry bag.

"Don't forget your vitamin," I say. Her vitamin, my euphemism for the Pill, which she started taking last month after "officially" reaching third base with Roger Sorenson, the "misunderstood" boy in her class with the long bangs and the snarl, who writes poetry and, according to Allison, passionate songs about the Iraq War, cultural imperialism, and love.

I finish arranging the room for our visit, not surprised that Marcella hasn't spent the time to make us feel welcome. She has never seen us as family. Of course some of that has to do with me. I should have visited more often. In the last few years we've only been out four or five times, for short, hurry-up weekends, or the rare Christmas. I should have invited them to St. Paul more than the Thanksgiving when my father showed up alone on his way to Manitoba in search of the elusive yellow-billed loon. Maybe I should have gone with him. Or we could have just taken a drive out to some lake and looked at whatever birds might have been out there. Why didn't I do that?

I head downstairs, where simulated explosions blast from the TV, as Paul takes out his new, adolescent hostility on the colored shadows flitting around the screen.

"Paul," I say. "Will you turn that down, please? Paul?"

He picks up the remote and pushes the volume button.

"Thank you," I say, as I turn and head down the dark hallway toward my father's bedroom.

At the end of the hall, the bathroom door opens and Marcella comes out dressed in men's pajamas that are too big for her. She has let her hair down and is brushing out its kinks, exposing the gray roots above the chestnut dye-job.

"Linda," she whispers. "What are you doing down here?"

"I was thinking I'd say good night to Dad."

"I told you. He's sleeping."

"But I haven't seen him. I thought it would be a good time."

"Well," she says, "we don't want to wake him."

"You know what, Marcella?" I say, stifling the expletives that suddenly pop in my head. "He's my father and I would really like to just go in and see him. I'll be quiet, okay?"

She squeezes out one of her disapproving sighs. "All right," she says. "Go in."

I open the door and go inside. A dim night-light fills the room with a murky orange glow. My father is propped up in a hospital bed with silver railings. It's in a different place than his old bed, away from the windows, where he liked to wake up in the morning light. His head tilts toward his right shoulder, in the same direction as the sagging right side of his face. He has lost some hair, and his belly isn't nearly as large as the last time I saw him. Marcella has followed me into the room and is now standing beside me, tucking the blanket in by his foot. On the other side of the bed an old, drab quilt is draped over a small cot, undoubtedly where Marcella sleeps at night, devoted nurse-wife that she is.

"He's doing better," Marcella says.

"Better than what?"

"Than he was."

I reach out and touch his hair. It's greasy, unwashed. "Good night, Daddy. I'll see you tomorrow. Okay?"

As I leave the room I close the door behind me, ignoring Marcella and her disapproving glare. She can have him now in their strange orange room. She probably deserves it, serving the Lord all those years, and now sacrificing whatever happiness she probably wouldn't have felt anyway to be by my father's side during these difficult times. Some people find an inexplicable joy in suffering.

Upstairs Allison is curled up on the bed with her eyes closed and her earphones in her ears. She started listening to Shakespeare when her father, an English professor at the University of Minnesota, walked out on us. She wants so desperately to connect with him that somehow even *Coriolanus* is interesting to her.

When I crawl into bed beside her, I realize that she is sound asleep, the little voices in her ears singing an iambic lullaby.

What am I doing? I ask myself. This is the question every compulsive failure asks. And then of course repeats: what the hell am I doing? Is this what I wanted? Maybe I need to suffer like Marcella.

Brian, my separation, is probably in Minneapolis tonight with some leggy blond, a Sonja or an Ilse, who chuckles every time a clever witticism squirms its way through his lips.

In therapy Dr. Hutchins took Brian's side almost from the start, and together they worked me over, exposing every fault, as if they were geologists digging up and analyzing my fragile inner core. Brian enjoyed those sessions, and it began to seem as if he were there to get validation from a professional that I alone was the cause of his unhappiness.

What is it in me that causes unhappiness in men? My father was always disappointed in my lack of interest in his bird-watching, and in my need to get out of here, to leave this all behind, as if forsaking everything he'd worked so hard to attain. I know he was proud of me and my independence. He told me so. But was I proud of him? Did I ever tell him, or Brian for that matter, that I was impressed by something he had done?

The next morning I wake up before anyone and go down to the Hinky Dinky to stock up on some much-needed groceries. When I get back, Paul is up, playing one of those games again.

"Where'd you go?" he asks.

"I went to the store. You want an omelet?"

"No, thanks," he says. "Just cereal."

He doesn't look at me during this exchange, and I decide to end this behavior now, wishing I'd done it from the start. I set the bags on the kitchen counter and head back into the living room. "Paul, I'm going to ask you something, and you're not going to like it. But I want you to turn that off and pack it up and put it away for the rest of the trip."

"What?"

"I want you to spend time with me. With family."

"Can't I just take a break?"

"No. I want you to do what I ask. Don't fight me on this one, okay?" I can see the fight begin to take shape in his round face, the way he sets his jaw just like his father.

"But . . . ," he says.

"Come on in and help me make breakfast."

"I only want cereal."

"I don't care what you want. We are going into the kitchen and we are going to cook breakfast."

I reach behind the TV and yank at some cords. The screen goes blank. "You're with family. It's time to act like it."

"What's the point?"

"That's a good question," I say. "And you know what? That won't be the last time you ask that."

Paul gets up and follows me into the kitchen, where he serves himself and sits at the table, slurping the milk from his bowl, while I stir Egg-Beaters for Dad, and prepare the pancake batter for the rest of us. He has a lot to learn, my son, and I'm doing my best not to teach it all to him right now.

Allison comes downstairs in her old U of M sweatshirt, and says, "Good morrow, sweet lady. Good morrow, gentle sir."

"Good morrow, dumbass," Paul says.

"Hey," I say, turning to him, "what did I say about that language?"

"Don't worry about him, Linda," Allison says, opening the refrigerator. "He doesn't understand us." She takes out a carton of orange juice and says, "So what's for breakfast?"

"Pancakes."

"Oh, can I help?" she says.

Paul looks up from the table and shakes his head.

Allison grabs a glass from the cupboard and pours the orange juice. "Where's Grampa?"

"He and Marcella haven't gotten up yet."

Paul stands and puts his bowl in the sink. "Can he even get up?" he says.

"Of course," I say. "The doctor says he should be up as much as possible."

Just as we are about to serve breakfast, Marcella comes into the kitchen with her hair pulled back into a bun. "Oh, my goodness. Look at this," she says.

"Paul," I say, "why don't you set the table."

Allison wipes her hands and says, "Good morning, Grandma M. Where's Grampa?"

"Oh, he's still in bed. I already gave him his sponge bath and he had his morning helping of Ensure. And now he's watching TV."

"What?" I say. "He can come out here and have breakfast with us, can't he?"

"Well," she says, "in his fragile state, it's best for him to remain in bed."

"Marcella," I say, now trying to sound conciliatory. "I talked to Dr. Reed last week and he said that with proper rehab, Dad could be up and walking freely in a couple months. What's the point of staying in bed?"

Marcella straightens up and takes a deep breath. "The point of him staying in bed, Linda, is to make him comfortable and perhaps prolong his life."

"I can't believe this," I say, slamming the spatula on the countertop.

I leave her and the children in the kitchen and go into my father's room. He is propped up in his pajamas, watching *The Price is Right*. The curtains are drawn, and the room is still aglow with that sad orange light. He turns his head as I come up to his bedside. His right eye is almost completely shut, and the entire side of his face sags like wax that has softened in the sun.

"Hi, Dad," I say. "Good morning."

"La . . . Laverna?" he says, struggling to get the word out.

"No, Daddy. It's Linda."

"Li . . . Linda?"

"Yes. Your daughter."

"Linda," he says, tears filling his eyes, as he raises his left arm. "Linda."

I bend forward and take up his slack body. His left arm surprises me with its strength as it pulls me into him. "Hi, Daddy," I say, stifled by the rank smell of his body, his hair greasy, with dry flakes stuck in the thin gray strands.

"Let's liven up this place, shall we?" I go to the window and open the curtain. "Wow, look at that! Winter's over, Daddy. It's spring now. Migration time."

"Linda?" he says.

"Yes, Daddy. What is it?"

"Where . . . where ith you mudduh?"

"Mother? Well, she's gone. She died, Dad."

"What?" To see his face now, and the startling grief, as he relives the mourning all over again, is shocking. I hadn't thought about that. Everything that has happened in the past ten or twenty years has vanished from his memory.

I put my hand on his shoulder. "I'm sorry." I yank a couple of Kleenex from the box on the nightstand and wipe his wet cheeks.

Marcella walks into the room and closes the door behind her. My father turns his head in her direction. "Laverna?" he slurs.

"No, Sam," she says. "It's just me, your wife."

"My wife?"

"Marcella," she says.

The crowd cheers on the TV as a bald man jumps up and down. I pick up the remote and click it off. It's quiet now and I can feel Marcella's eyes on me as I set the remote down.

"I am doing the best I can," she says. "I'm all alone here."

"I know, Marcella," I say. "And I'm sorry. I know you've had it rough. And I know you love him. But I don't know how happy he is, stuck in here."

"Do you think he knows any better?" she asks.

"I don't know. Maybe a part of him would like to get out of this bed, take a shower. Maybe that's what he wants. Who wants to be in bed all day?"

"And how do I give him a shower? I can't hold him up."

"I don't know. You get help. He could really improve, Marcella. That's what Dr. Reed said. He needs to get up and start moving."

"I don't have the strength."

"What if I hire a nurse who can come in here and clean him up, take him into the clinic for rehab? Would that be okay with you?"

"Before this happened," she says, her eyes filling with tears, "he was out of the house for days on end. And I never knew where he was."

"Looking for birds?"

She nods. "He didn't want you to know, because he was supposed to let up. But he was still going at it, and here I was, all alone in this house, waiting for him to come back."

"You could have gone with him."

"And do what, sit in the car for hours? Hike through marsh and prickers? Just for the chance to see some bird?"

"Yeah," I say. "I know."

"I don't know why he was so obsessed with those birds."

"They made him happy."

"I suppose so," she says. "But I wanted to make him happy."

My father is staring up at her with his warped gaze. "And now," she says, with a sad ironic chuckle that turns into tears, "he doesn't know who the hell I am."

"Give him a reason to know who you are," I tell her. "We need to reboot, you know, give him a new life. Don't you think? Marcella, he won't leave anymore, not without you."

"Oh, he's going to leave," she says.

I immediately understand what she's saying. "Yes, but until that time he should be happy, shouldn't he? Let's get him up and moving. Give him a shower, puts some clothes on him. What do you say?"

"I don't know." Her voice is so full of doubt that the words hardly make their way out of her mouth.

"Listen, Marcella. I'm sorry. I mean, I know how I can be."

"That's okay," she says. "I can be that way too." About this, she smiles at me and I smile back. It is the first positive connection we've ever made.

"Who are you?" my father asks.

Marcella shakes her head. "I'm Marcella, you old coot. I'm your godforsaken wife."

"Wife?"

I go out to the kitchen and tell Paul to come with me.

"Why?"

"I need your help with something. Come on, Allison," I say, turning back to the bedroom. "Say good morning to your grampa."

Allison comes into the room and says, "Hi, Grampa." She hesitates and tries to smile, suddenly apprehensive.

"Hi, dear," he replies, like he knows who she is.

I say, "Daddy, this is Allison. Hasn't she grown?"

"Are you in school?" he asks.

"No, it's spring break, Grampa."

Paul comes into the room and says, with a flash of confidence that is new to me, "Hey Gramps, what's up? It's Paul. You remember me, don't you?"

"Paul? Little Paul?"

"I'm not so little anymore," Paul says.

"Are you in school?" Dad asks.

"No, Gramps, it's spring break."

"Hey, Dad, how's this for a plan," I say. "We get you into the shower and then put some clothes on you and you can sit at the window and look at birds."

"Birds?"

"Yes."

"Where?"

"Just here, Daddy. In the backyard."

He nods, pushing his head awkwardly back and forth.

"We're going to help you out of bed and into the bathroom."

"I can walk," he mutters.

Marcella says, "He always tells me that, but he can only stand on his left leg. His right one doesn't have any strength."

Paul, Allison, and I sit him up and help him out of the bed. This is my father, the farm boy who became a high-school football star before enlisting in the Air Force and then working the rail lines. His bones are still thick as lumber, and his frame is considerable. Paul takes after him. You can see it in the pictures of Dad at thirteen, the large jaw and forehead, the deep chest and broad shoulders. Marcella watches cautiously as we work our way into the bathroom and set Dad on the toilet. The foul smell is almost overwhelming, even with the sponge baths Marcella gives him. Paul is amazingly good-natured about the whole thing. Allison moves out of the bathroom and says something to Marcella back in the bedroom.

"Here, will you help me take off his pajamas?" I say.

"What?" Paul says. "I mean, *Mom!*"

"Just grab here and pull. Daddy, I need you to help us now. Can you lift your leg a little bit?"

Paul and I pull his pajamas off, leaving him slumped over on the toilet seat. His pale, naked body startles me, the rolls of skin sagging down his chest and stomach, the mass of white pubic hair around his shriveled, uncircumcised penis. I turn away, keeping my eyes on Paul as best I can.

"So now what do we do?" Paul says.

"I don't know," I say. "I think you might have to get in there with him."

"Where?"

"The bathtub."

"What?"

"How else can we stand him up?"

"I can stand," my father mumbles.

"I know you can, Daddy. But we don't want you falling down."

"I'm not taking my clothes off," Paul says. "No way."

"Well, let's get him in there, and then you can take them off behind the curtain. I won't look."

"Nope," he says. "Sorry. This isn't going to happen."

Allison leans into the bathroom. "Paul," she says, "for once will you just think about someone else?"

"Why don't *you* do it?" he asks.

"Paul!" she says.

He takes in a breath and closes his lips, looking down at his grandfather. "Close the door," he says, turning to Allison. "Just shut up and get out of here."

We struggle to get Dad up and into the tub. But once he's stable, Paul takes off his pants, leaving his T-shirt and underwear on. I reach in to turn on the water.

"Hot," Dad says. "Too hot."

As Paul keeps Dad's right side stable, I squeeze a dab of shampoo into his left hand. He puts it on Dad's head and begins massaging it into his scalp. I look in to see how everything is going, and Paul becomes agitated.

"Mom, close the curtain," he says. "I've got it."

"Soap," Dad says.

"Here you go, Gramps," Paul says. "He's washing his body, Mom. He's doing pretty good, actually."

After he's done, Paul dries him off, and we help him into the bedroom where Allison and Marcella have picked out a sweater and a pair of trousers. While we slip him into his clothes, Marcella strips the bed and begins a load of wash.

Dad sits at the dining room table, while Allison, who is getting more comfortable around him, helps him with his food. Paul has come out of his gloomy shell and talks on and on about football and the kung fu class he took during the winter. Dad seems to be able to track the conversation, only occasionally asking Paul who he is and if he's in school. At one point during the meal, he mutters to Allison, "Linda, don't forget your homework."

"I'm Allison, Grampa," she replies, "and I do my homework every day."

I make a pot of tea, and we help Dad out onto the back porch, where he can sit in the sunshine and listen to the birds. I let Paul stay inside to watch TV, while Allison talks on the phone to Roger. Marcella stands in the kitchen peering at us through the window.

Dad leans back in his chair and closes his eyes. A lot has been lost between us, I know. So I fill him in on Brian, the kids, my job. I ramble for a while, telling him how I almost got fired for writing a nasty letter to the editor of the *St. Paul Gazette*, and how one of Paul's teachers got thrown in jail for writing bad checks. Then I tell him the story of how Brian decided it was over, how it wasn't me, it was just a feeling he had, something nagging at him, and so he flew down to Costa Rica for two weeks to sit on a beach and think about things. When he came back, his scalp was pink through his thinning hair, and the tops of his feet were riddled with blisters. He lay on the bed, suffering a mild sunstroke, and as I caressed his skin with aloe vera, he started crying. He wouldn't tell me why. He just cried and then fell asleep. The next morning I woke up to him stuffing his bags, still not saying anything. I didn't say anything either. I just lay there and watched him go.

My father tries to nod, his head making little jerking motions.

"It's good to see you, Dad," I say. "It's good to see you again."

"*Sshhh!!!*" he says, leaning forward. A cackle stretches across the sky. It sounds like a screen door creaking on its hinges. My father cocks his head and closes his eyes. "Is . . . is it spring?" he mumbles.

"Yes it is, Dad."

"The cranes," he says, the *r* sounding more like a *w*. *"Duh cwanes."*

"Yes," I say. "They're migrating."

He opens his eyes and looks at me. "Let's go."

"Whoa, whoa, Dad." I almost laugh. "Where do you want to go?"

"Cranes."

"I don't think that's a good idea, Daddy."

He sits back with a sigh and closes his eyes.

"I'm sorry," I say. "It's just maybe not a good time right now." As I say this nothing feels right. It's like the words are coming from someone else, and I'm sitting here watching those words leave her mouth, and I'm filled with disgust. If not now, then when? Isn't it always *not now? Not now this, not now that.* I think about the word now. It's not a word I've paid a lot of attention to.

A crane's call echoes through the distance. My father sits still, listening, waiting for another one.

"Hell," I say. "Why not?" I stand up and put my hand on my father's shoulder. "You want to go see cranes, then we'll go see cranes."

I pull open the sliding glass door and go into the house. Marcella is in their bedroom, putting clean sheets on his bed. "What?" she says. "No, Linda. This is going too far too fast."

"Yeah, you're probably right. But it's what he wants. You know those birds will be gone in a day or two. Come on, Marcella. Why don't you come along with us?"

She grabs a pillow and starts jamming it into a pillowcase. "I don't want to look at birds."

"Well, you're invited," I say, leaving the room. "I'd like you to come."

Allison leans into the hall with the phone pressed to her ear. "Where you going?"

"Out," I say. "You're coming with us. Get your jacket."

"Okay," she says, and then turns back to the phone. "Roger, yeah, I gotta split. I don't know."

I go into the living room and tell Paul. He looks up from the TV and says, "Do I have to go?"

"No, you don't have to do anything," I tell him. "Now go outside and help Grampa."

I open the front closet, surprised to find all of my father's old jackets still hanging in there, and unlike any other place in the house, the familiar scent of my childhood rushes back. I feel as if I could just scoot in and close the door and those years would return. My mother is in there somewhere with her funny, sputtery laugh and those clompy feet that descended squarely on the ground, and my father too, the tough, sometimes distant man who occasionally surrendered to his most surprising impulses.

Paul and Dad make their way through the kitchen and living room. "That's good, Grampa," Paul says. "Just a few more steps."

I grab the beige Dickies jacket my father used to wear when he shoveled the walk in winter, and hand it to Paul. "Here, put this on him."

"Wha . . ." my father says. "What?"

"Daddy," I say slowly and a bit too loudly. "We are going out for a drive."

Paul and I pull and tug the jacket onto Dad as he wobbles

back and forth, trying to maintain his balance. I take his left hand and Paul his right, and we lead him to the front door.

"Allison, honey!" I bark. "Come on."

"I'll be right down!"

"Yeah, right," Paul says.

We open the door, and a breeze kicks up from the south. The new leaves on the giant oak in the front yard whisper their displeasure.

We struggle getting him down the steps. The right side of his body hangs slack and lifeless. Paul and I support him as he shuffles to the car. He is methodical, his gaze fixed on the pavement before him. We make it around the car and Paul opens the door and we lower Dad into the front seat.

Allison eventually emerges from the house in the sweater her father recently brought back from Ireland. Her hair is brushed back, and she's put on makeup. What is she thinking?

"I'm sorry I held you guys up," she says, with a genuineness that tries my patience.

"That's all right," Paul says. "We were born to wait for you."

As his father says, "We have a boy whose ass is smarter than his brain."

As I turn the key in the ignition, Marcella comes out of the house in a violet winter coat and approaches the car with a frown on her face.

"Are you coming with us?" I say.

Allison scoots to the middle of the backseat, and Marcella gets in and slams the door.

"You okay, Grandma M?" Allison says.

"Comfy-cozy," she says.

I pull the car out and head south of town before turning west on

Highway 30 toward Alda. Thousands of people from all over the world come here, to this small place in the middle of nowhere, at this time of year to see an annual event people have marveled over for centuries, probably, and, even though it is only miles from my childhood home, and even though my father used to beg me to go with him, I've never been to see the migration of the great sandhill cranes. Hundreds of thousands of these birds fly north from the Gulf up to the Arctic tundra. They make a pit stop here on the Platte River where they refill their tanks for their last, long stretch home.

My father sits in the front seat beside me staring at the dashboard. Outside, the heather bounces up purple on the roadside, and birds of all sorts show their romantic coloring. But Dad doesn't. He's forgotten what we'll be seeing.

"Where are we going?" Paul says.

"For a drive."

Allison leans forward and says. "Can we stop by the mall on the way home?"

"Honey, no."

As I turn onto South Alda Road and approach the Wood River Bridge, more and more cars fill the road, with license plates from Tennessee, New Mexico, Washington. Paul starts reading them out loud.

"What are they all doing here?" Allison says.

"Same thing we're doing."

"What, going for a drive?" Paul says.

"Well," I say. "You'll see."

"Every year at this time," Marcella says, tired of the kids' questions, "the sandhill cranes migrate up through here. We are going to look at them."

"Oh beautiful," Paul says, disappointed.

Cars are parked up and down the roadside. On the other side of the river, hundreds of people with binoculars are gathered on a large concrete viewing deck.

"What are they looking at?" Paul asks.

We pass the jammed parking lot and go back a ways, following RVs and tour buses onto dirt roads that surround vast unplowed fields of corn and milo. "What's going on?" Paul asks. "Why are we out here?"

"I don't know," I say. "I'm just following this RV."

Out among the dried, splintered cornstalks, thousands of large gray birds rustle around, foraging in the field.

"Wow," Paul says. "What are those things?"

"Those are the cranes," Marcella says, somehow not losing patience with him.

"Dad," I say, raising my hand in front of him, pointing out the window. "Look. Look out there, Dad."

Allison leans forward, touching his shoulder. "They're birds, Grampa. Cranes. Thousands of them."

He tries to turn his head, but he can only get to where he is seeing the doorframe or maybe the rearview mirror. I turn the car and angle off the road so he can look at them straight on. They are large birds, easily three feet tall, and they're gray—ashy, earthy gray. A reddish mask covers their eyes, fading into a drab gray toward the bill. A bushy pompadour sticks out of their behinds. With Dad's poor eyesight, I'm not sure he can see them.

"They're cranes, Daddy. The sandhill cranes. Right out there."

"Oh," he says, searching into the blurry world beyond the car.

"They're kind of weird-looking," Paul says.

"Nothing is weird-looking," Allison says. "It's just that *you think* it's weird."

"So," Paul says. "Same thing."

While they ramble on in back, I watch my father. He hasn't seen the birds yet and it pains me that I have forgotten his glasses or even his binoculars. "You see them, Daddy? They're right out there, just like you remember. Like you used to tell me about. Remember?"

"Of . . . course," he slurs.

"They're prehistoric-looking, Grampa," Allison says.

"Gray," he says. "With . . . with . . . a rusty . . . belly." He lifts his left hand and touches his stomach. He is describing them, but I can tell that he hasn't seen them.

In the paper it said that as the sun goes down, the birds return in massive flocks to the river, singing their strange songs and splashing in the water. I put the car in reverse and pull out, around a giant tour bus with Missouri plates.

"Where are we going, Mom?" Allison asks.

"I don't know."

"They're kind of cool," Paul says. "Kind of like modern ptero-dactyls with little beaks or something."

I turn around and head back toward the river. "When was the last time you went bird-watching, Dad?"

"Huh?"

"Bird-watching?"

"Yes," he says.

"When did you go last? You know, the last time?"

He looks up, and I can see his thought forming on his droop-ing face. "Last . . . time," he says. "Yes. Last . . . time."

"Are we going home now?" Allison asks.

"No," I say.

As I turn onto a small dirt road that runs along the river, I glance over at my father, who is now crying.

"What's wrong, Daddy?" I ask. "What's wrong?"

"Upland . . . sandpiper," he says.

"What?"

"Bluethroat. Red-breasted . . . merganser." And now the tears are rolling down his face.

"Oh, it's okay, Daddy. It's okay." I look at Allison in the rearview mirror. "Allison, honey, could you get a Kleenex and help your grampa please?"

"Last . . . time," he says.

The horde of cars and buses has disappeared behind us as we squirrel along the south bank of the river. Giant cottonwoods and sycamores separate us from the water. I find a small turnoff and park the car.

"What are we doing here?" Paul asks.

"Come on," I say. "Let's get Grampa out of the car."

"What?" Marcella says.

"Where are we going?" Paul asks.

"Paul, just help your grandfather. We are going down to the river."

Marcella leans forward and says, "I don't think that's a good idea."

"That's fine," I say. "But he wants to see the birds, and I think this is a good spot."

We pull Dad out of the car and help him across the dirt road. "Are you all right, Daddy?" I ask. "Are you warm enough?"

He attempts a nod, and then says, "The river."

"Right, Daddy," I say. "The river. The Platte River." Can he see it, or just hear it? Maybe he smells it. But I'm surprised, because it's still a good distance off.

We struggle down from the road, through thick brush and marsh and the furry cattails Paul keeps calling "hot dog plants."

"That time of year that mayst in me behold," Allison says, fiddling with a reed she has picked up. "When yellow leaves, or none, or few do hang."

"Oh, no," Paul says. "Not the Shakespeare."

"Upon those boughs which shake against the cold."

"Please," Paul says. "Stop torturing me!"

Allison continues ahead of us, mumbling the rest to herself.

As we approach the water, Dad's body eases up. He relaxes a bit. The water swirls and crawls along, and we're all quiet. Something about water I have noticed, when first meeting up with it—a lake, a river, a sea—there is something to take in, some respect granted before people move on to whatever they were going to do in the first place. Even Paul looks out at the silty water, wondering where it is all going, probably, or where it came from.

"Come on," I say. "Let's clear some of this brush here and sit down."

"It's kind of wet," Allison says.

"Well," I tell her, "we're going to be here for a little while, and if we're standing here, the birds probably won't come our way."

"What birds?" Paul asks.

Allison shoots him a look. "The cranes, silly."

"Oh, beautiful," Paul says. "Why do we have to see more cranes?"

"Listen," I say. "You can go back to the car if you want. But we are going to stay here with your grandfather."

"Fine," Paul says, turning away. "I'm getting cold anyway."

"Paul," Allison says, "get back here and help us clear a spot for Grampa."

With that he turns around, and with a sizable frown, begins stomping the ground around us, leveling the reeds and matting down a comfortable place for us to sit.

"Honey," I say. "If you're cold, you can go back to the car."

"No," Paul says. "I'm fine."

Eventually Marcella arrives, her hands full of clover and milkweed. "I thought I'd pick some flowers," she says. "Look at these."

"They're beautiful," Allison says.

"It's surprising how much is blooming already."

"If you're going to be here, Marcella, you're going to have to sit down. We have to be inconspicuous."

"Oh," she says. "Is it wet?"

"It's not too bad," Allison says.

"I just don't want to get my coat messy," Marcella says, before crouching down beside Paul.

My father has been holding on to Allison this whole time, staring out at the river, trying to focus on something. The sun is slipping behind the trees down the river to the west, and above us the sky is turning a crimson red. The breeze calms to an occasional flutter.

"We might see some birds, Daddy," I whisper.

"Birds?"

"Sandhill cranes."

He jerks his head into a nod and says, "Ka . . . kar . . . karrooo."

"What, Daddy? What are you trying to say?"

From out of nowhere a crane flies overhead, and then another one, nervous, alert, scouting out a spot on the river. And then horns start blaring, like car horns, and then silence.

Paul whispers, "Mom, look. Here they come."

We look back toward the trees behind us. Through the new-forming leaves, a blurry spotted shadow moves across the sky, a giant, dark rolling cloud, and then a clamor of trumpets, rattles, cries, and cackles that shake the marsh beneath us.

"Daddy," I whisper, placing my hand on his shoulder. "The cranes are coming. They're coming right over us."

"Sam," Marcella whispers. "Honey, look up, up above us."

He tries to turn around, but his head stops when his eyes reach mine, and then he sets his empty stare onto me.

"Here they come, Dad."

Over the crest of the cottonwoods, the cranes—thousands of cranes—flap their enormous wings, pushing on the air, until just above us, where they stretch out and open their wings into a glide, howling and wailing to each other, before sweeping the sky and spiraling downward onto the river.

"Wow," Paul whispers.

"Karrooo!" the birds cry out. "Karrooo!"

My father turns toward the water and closes his eyes.

"Where late the sweet birds sing," Allison says, the words hushed from a deep sigh.

My father opens his eyes and scans the river. His eyelids work at opening and closing.

"Do you see the cranes, Daddy?" I whisper, as they preen and prance out in the shallow water in front of us.

"Who are you?" my father says.

"I'm Linda, Dad," I tell him. "I'm your daughter."

"Linda?" he says.

"Yes, Linda. And today I took you out here so we could see the cranes."

"Oh," he murmurs. "The cranes."

"You were right, all those years," I say. "They're beautiful, Daddy. They're just beautiful."

"They're . . . they're on their way . . ." he says, not completing his thought.

"Yes," I say. "Yes they are. They're on their way."

"Karrooo," he whispers. "Karrooo."

Alex Mindt was born and raised in Edmonds, Washington. He is a graduate of the Columbia University MFA program, winner of the Pushcart Prize, and an award-winning filmmaker. He has worked as a teacher, salesman, carpenter, nanny, truck driver, social worker, strawberry picker, mason's assistant, birdhouse builder, voiceover actor and has lived in every region of the country. He currently teaches at the Gotham Writers' Workshop, and lives in New York City with his wife and two children.

Visit the author's website at www.alexmindt.com.